My first novel,
Be kind !
Love
Fran x

The Mirrored Garden

The Mirrored Garden

FRAN FOSTER

First edition 2021

Book design by Publishing Push

ISBN 978-1-80227-292-5 (paperback)
ISBN 978-1-80227-293-2 (ebook)

Published by PublishingPush.com

Typeset using Atomik ePublisher from Easypress Technologies

The Family Tree

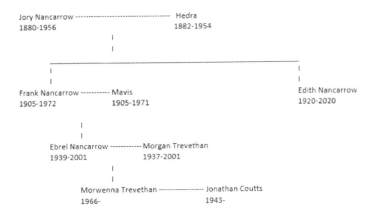

Jory Nancarrow ----------------------------------- Hedra
1880-1956   1882-1954

Frank Nancarrow ----------- Mavis   Edith Nancarrow
1905-1972   1905-1971   1920-2020

Ebrel Nancarrow ------------ Morgan Trevethan
1939-2001   1937-2001

Morwenna Trevethan ----------------- Jonathan Coutts
1966-   1943-

Chapter 1

The Lockdown

The silence of the morning was broken by the clatter of mail landing on the doormat. Morwenna awoke to the queasiness of dread and damp with perspiration. During the night she had dreamt of Jonathan. The air was sharp and cold in her nostrils and there came a jolt to her chest, a long fall and finally, a blanket of blackness. She gasped for breath, alone in her bedroom in Bath, with her husband's distorted features still fresh in her mind. The frightening image faded and her inner voice spoke firmly. Just a few weeks to go and he would be back from Australia.

Morwenna had endured a very quiet three months since the lockdown of March 2020. Jonathan had flown out to Australia to see family in February and he had become stranded due to the corona virus pandemic. He had decided it was wiser and safer to stay put, until things were back to normal. Little did they know, at the time, that nothing would be remotely *normal* for over two years.

Through the bedroom window, she glimpsed a gull soar then stoop across the sky, sadly devoid of vapour trails.

'Please fly home safely,' she whispered to his photograph. 'It will be hard for me to carry on until things are as they *should be*.'

Morwenna lingered and fought the urge to continue lying there. She had come to rely on her husband over the last ten years. She recalled her visceral dismay in finding herself separated from Jonathan, on other side of the planet. She chastised herself and her feelings of insecurity.

Jonathan would have told her to enjoy the moment rather than regretting what could have been.

Their flat in Bath was large and lovely, under normal circumstances, but the property had no garden. It had been stifling during the unusual heat of April, May and June. Normally Morwenna walked daily in The Royal Victoria Park, which was right on her doorstep, but it had been closed for most of April and May. Now the park had re-opened, it was so packed with walkers and joggers that she was reluctant to go there. She was shameful of her fear of corona virus in comparison to the bravery of front-line workers. Morwenna encouraged herself and others to be kinder to themselves, and she acknowledged that she had never been good with illness.

The ability to entertain herself endlessly was one of her strengths but by June, she had read every book in the house and watched all that TV streaming had to offer. She had written to, or called friends and family members but indoor meetings were still prohibited. Conversations, even with good friends, had become stilted due to lack of news to share. She was frankly bored and there was still no end in sight. Like most people, she was glued to the television for news of the pandemic and some hint that the lockdown would be lifted and any semblance of normal life could return. She felt compelled to watch the evening corona briefings in their entirety before beginning supper preparation. Meals had become slightly haphazard because of her reluctance to go out for extra provisions during the week, relying on one large online order being delivered once every two weeks. This meant she often ran out of basic ingredients and her food became somewhat unconventional.

Delivery of post was a little hit and miss due too, although Morwenna had received a few letters from Harriet Duncan, an old school friend, who shared a propensity to send handwritten letters. Harriet had retired from her role as a paediatrician just before the pandemic. She became quickly frustrated moving from a busy job to lockdown, almost overnight, so she had returned to work for three months. Her friend was now convalescing after contracting corona virus and she had decided to finish work completely.

Once Morwenna coaxed her body out of bed, she ambled into the hallway. She noticed a rather old-fashioned envelope resting stiffly on the floor. She picked up the letter and stroked the good quality ivory paper, which was heavy and opulent. She loved the texture of expensive stationary. The address was typed, not handwritten, so certainly not from Harriet or other friends. It was not junk-mail as it was addressed to her personally, and oddly, in her maiden name, *Miss Morwenna Trevethan*. She had been married for a decade, so she rarely received mail in her former name now, and it was quite peculiar see it. She took the letter to her desk and opened it with a paper knife. Ordinarily she would have torn open the envelope, but she had a notion that there was something special and menacing about *this* letter. She glanced at the post mark: Truro and noted it had been posted ten days ago.

Drat the delay in post, she thought to herself. She then reflected that, had this been something really important, there were plenty of other ways to contact her.

The letter read as follows:

Dear Miss Trevethan,

Messers Kendal-Smalley require you to contact them as a matter of importance as you are named as a beneficiary in the last will and testament of Edith Nancarrow, who sadly passed away on 29th May 2020.

Please contact our Truro office at your earliest convenience.
Yours Sincerely

For a moment she stared at the letter and tilted her head. Her hands shook with no justification. She was an only-child and she had lost her parents, Ebrel and Morgan, many years before. She had never expected to become the beneficiary of *any* will after her mother and father died in 2001, in an airline disaster. They had been travelling on a post-retirement world-tour. Their plane from USA to Dominican Republic had crashed, killing all passengers. The suddenness of losing both of her parents had primed Morwenna to expect bad news when people contacted her without warning. She unconsciously expected things to go wrong and anticipated that phone calls or letters heralded a loss or tragedy.

She did not immediately recognise the name, *Edith Nancarrow,* except to register that Nancarrow was her mother's maiden-name. She had completed some research on her ancestors several years earlier and after a few minutes, she thought the name did ring a bell. Morwenna paused for a few seconds, pondering what to do next. With shivering hands, she fired up her lap-top and checked her family tree.

Morwenna had never got round to looking at the detail of the Nancarrows although she had researched the Treventhans more thoroughly. Using the genealogy website, she identified Edith as her mother's aunt.

She had researched her father's ancestry before meeting Jonathan. She hadn't done much with it since then, as he had no interest in family history and he had told her he preferred to *let sleeping dogs lie.* Her husband was a pragmatist. He gained his pleasures in the *here and now,* whereas Morwenna missed the anchor of a multigenerational family. Her parents and grandparents were dead and she had no siblings. Her life journey was like a flotsam and jetsam, as Jonathan called it in his Somerset parlance. She was buffeted by the prevailing tides and winds.

Edith Nancarrow had been her maternal grandfather's younger sister (significantly younger with her grandfather, Frank Nancarrow being born in 1905 and Edith being born in 1920). So, Edith was just over one hundred years old at the time of her death. A small amount of exploration satisfied Morwenna that Edith had been a spinster and childless herself. She had the vaguest recollection of her mother mentioning an aunt who lived in Porthleven, whom her mother had visited for holidays as a youngster. Morwenna had once asked her mother about Edith, but she had shut the conversation down, alluding to some ancient family argument. As a consequence, the subject was dropped. Otherwise, she knew nothing about the Nancarrows and her mother had never talked about Edith since.

It crossed her mind that this letter could be a scam, but this could be relatively easily checked. She scrutinized the sheet of paper, back and front, like a sleuth. Having read the communication more than five times, she could discover no further clues.

Morwenna felt sorry she had never been in touch with 'Great Aunt Edith', especially since Edith seemingly had no closer relatives. She had a habit of *collecting* old ladies and helping them out as much as possible. It seemed quite sad and ironic that she knew nothing of Edith Nancarrow. She worked herself up into a groundless state of guilt by midmorning. Although the sense of shame did not completely overwhelm her curiosity. She didn't want to appear *too* keen by phoning the solicitor straight away. Her delay in making the call was somewhat unnecessary, since the letter had already taken well over a week to arrive!

Morwenna sat cautiously looking at the phone for quite a while before dialling the number. The pulse in her temples quickened as the call connected. She had the sort of feeling one has, just before embarking on a course of action that, once started, cannot be reversed. She feared a decision which may lead to an outcome later regretted. Typically, the call went straight to an answering service- *Thank you for calling Kendal-Smalley Solicitors. Due to the corona pandemic, we are working limited hours. This answering machine is checked periodically. Please leave your name and number and we will get back to you.*

Morwenna emitted a huge breath of relief. She flopped her head against the back of the chair and let her arms dangle for a moment. Then, she left her details as requested and settled down with a cup of tea to steady her nerves. Normally she would have gone out for a short walk at this hour of the morning, but she was far too intrigued to risk missing the return call. She let her thoughts wander to see if she could retrieve anything further about Edith Nancarrow. Given that Morwenna's mother had very few relatives indeed, it struck her that it was quite strange that she knew almost nothing about her great aunt. Morwenna was an only-child, as was her mother, hence it was even more curious that Edith had never been mentioned. Frank Nancarrow, Morwenna's late grandfather had been Edith's only sibling.

After her parent's tragic deaths in 2001, Morwenna had contacted everyone in her mother's address book to invite them to the memorial service, but Edith was not listed and she had assumed there were no surviving members of the Nancarrow family. Her grandparents Frank and Mavis Nancarrow had died in the early 1970's when Morwenna had been a young child. She hadn't been close to them.

Why was Great Aunt Edith never mentioned? she ruminated, as she ambled to the kitchen and sat at the neatly-laid table. She studied the familiar backdrop of her home and concluded that her days were far too monotonous. *Humdrum*, Jonathan would have called it, in his old-fashioned vernacular. How she missed his little sayings, now he wasn't here. Maybe the solicitor would tell her something which would shake things up. She longed for some excitement.

She flinched when the phone rang and hesitated for a moment before speaking.

'Hello,' Morwenna whispered. Her voice was fragile.

'Good morning. This is Felicity Cartwright, from Kendal-Smalley Solicitors. May I speak to Miss Morwenna Trevethan?' the caller uttered, in a clipped fashion.

'Yes, Morwenna *Coutts* Speaking, Trevethan was my maiden-name.'

'Sorry Mrs Coutts, I just need to check your date of birth to ensure we have traced the correct person?'

She detailed her date of birth, 24th June 1966 and Felicity Cartwright confirmed that she had identified the right individual.

'I am very sorry to inform you that your great aunt, Edith Nancarrow, has passed away,' said the woman. She followed with the typical trite platitudes people use when dealing with the bereaved. Morwenna curbed an uncharacteristic impulse to urge Miss Cartwright to *get to the point*.

'I am sorry for the slight delay in informing you,' continued the caller, 'but it was difficult to locate you, as your last address on our documentation, appears to be your late parents' home in Yorkshire. I hope you understand we had to authorise the funeral to go ahead.'

'Please don't concern yourself,' replied Morwenna. 'I never met my great-aunt and I didn't know I would benefit from her will.'

Morwenna was not a character who would accept sympathy, nor any other act of kindness, when none was due. Although, she did not explicitly state that she had barely heard of Edith Nancarrow, before today.

Miss Cartwright explained that she was the secretary at Kendal-Smalley Solicitors and that Angela Smalley was the solicitor dealing with the case. Miss Smalley requested that Morwenna meet with her in person. This was a slightly strange request, as the country was in the middle of a pandemic. People were being encouraged not to travel too far from home and use remote communicate methods as much as possible. Surely the solicitor could deal with probate and dispose of any assets without face-to-face contact. However, the secretary continued very persistently stating that Mrs Coutts was the *sole* beneficiary. She would find a visit, in person, essential as the assets were rather *substantial* and would require a period of review before disposal. This process was expected to take a number of weeks.

Morwenna pointed out that she could not book into a hotel due to lockdown restrictions. The caller informed her that arrangements had been made for her to stay at Edith's house. Apparently, the housekeeper, who had more recently acted as the old lady's nurse, was still residing at *Gwedr Iowarth*. This was the name of Edith's home, which was located a few minutes' walk from Porthleven in Cornwall. Morwenna felt embarrassed to ask about the approximate value of the estate, especially at this early stage. Finally, she gave in and agreed make arrangements to travel to Cornwall in early July.

Presently Morwenna's burdens drifted away. She threw open the sash window and observed the frantic scene below. Runners and skateboarders dashed through the park and hectic dogs chased one another. This trip would be an interesting distraction and an ideal excuse for an impromptu holiday. She had a brain-wave, she would contact Harriet and see if she would come too. Her friend had suffered quite badly with corona virus and had some symptoms of so called *long COVID syndrome*. She would probably benefit from a holiday by the sea. They might as well take advantage of the opportunity now, as the property would be sold once probate went through.

The following day Morwenna called the solicitor's office to check that the property was large enough to accommodate Harriet too. Felicity Cartwright laughed out loud and stated that the property was huge, and that social distancing would, *not be a problem.*

Morwenna bore a magnified sense of responsibility for things that went wrong around her. Jonathan frequently had to remind her not to be so sensitive. Without his intervention, she felt guilty when thinking about her good fortune. She had come into an unexpected inheritance and had the luxury of a holiday in the middle of an otherwise miserable period of world history.

Harriet, on the other hand, had no such reservations and agreed to come without hesitation. She was a very different person to Morwenna. Harriet's life had not been blighted by loss and she retained the support of her parents, even now. She was an eternal optimist and possessed an excitable and impulsive disposition. However currently, she was suffering with tiredness, muscle pains and pins and needles. Her GP had suggested she may have been more likely to have contracted COVID due to her biracial heritage but this did not account for her prolonged symptoms of the virus. She was sure a change of scene and some fresh air would do her a lot of good. She shared Morwenna's curiosity about the Nancarrow family feud, which gave an added frisson of excitement to their forthcoming adventure.

Chapter 2

Gwedr Iowarth

The two friends travelled down to Cornwall separately in early July. Stay-at-home travel restrictions had been lifted and it was now all about, *eat out to help out*. 'Eat out to help out' was a government-subsidy scheme aimed to promote eating in restaurants to help stimulate the economy. Although both women had been brought up in Yorkshire, Harriet was now living in mid-Wales and Morwenna in Bath. Public transport was highly problematic during the pandemic, so they both travelled by car and agreed to meet at the house. Morwenna planned to arrive mid-afternoon and Harriet in the early evening. Morwenna felt an unexpected sense of liberation as she drove on the open roads. As she entered the motorway, she sang at the top of her voice, drowning out the radio. Other drivers looked at her startled, as she celebrated of her release.

Felicity Cartwright had informed Morwenna that Ada Bray, the live-in housekeeper, would meet her at Gwedr Iowarth. Morwenna was concerned that the housekeeper was still living in the property and wondered if her long term association with Edith could prove a little tricky. It could become awkward when asking her to leave, once the house went on the market. Miss Cartwright re-assured Morwenna that Ada had been bequeathed a small cottage in Falmouth and a modest trust fund, so her future security should not be a problem. Also, she had agreed to supervise the clearance of the house prior to sale, which would be particularly useful. This partially put Morwenna's mind at rest, but she still worried that the dynamics between her and the staff member could prove highly problematic.

The solicitors had told her that the housekeeper had been an employee since she was fifteen years old and she was now in her early seventies. Apparently, Ada had come directly to *Gwedr Iowarth* from care in 1962, to become a live-in maid when the household still employed several servants. She must have been contented in her work, because she had stayed there to this day.

Morwenna was pondering these matters, as she drove down to Cornwall. Her mood slumped and she switched off the radio. She was still a little upset that Jonathan had not supported her decision to go to Porthleven in person. He worried about her health and the risk of contracting corona virus and favoured her asking the solicitors to deal with everything and have the house sold in her absence. In fact, he had spoken exceedingly forcefully from Australia on several occasions asking her to re-consider. She was also stubborn and was equally adamant that she would attend herself. She assured her husband that she would keep him updated with developments.

The roads were marvellously empty en route, due to the ongoing effects of the virus, and Morwenna made extremely good time. Considering she possessed a solely Cornish heritage, it was peculiar that she had never visited the county with her parents, when she was a child. Jonathan had advised against holidaying in Cornwall and Devon due to the crowds, especially in summer. She dropped down into Porthleven from Loe Bar, avoiding the town centre. It was a glorious warm and sunny day. The spectacular expanse of glittering water came upon her unexpectedly. Almost immediately after that, she swung around the hairpin bend into the long drive of *Gwedr Iowarth*.

At this moment she knew that she would never sell the house. How on earth was she going to persuade Jonathan to leave his beloved Bath?

The property was enormous, set in its own grounds with the grand entrance facing directly south, towards the sea. The terrace and garden were bordered by railings and a cliff edge beyond, plummeting to rocks below and small private beach. Morwenna was absolutely stunned.

Even in her limited experience of real estate, she realised this house would be worth a good deal of money. The upkeep costs would be phenomenal and her heart sank as she released, that although she and Jonathan were very comfortably off, there was very little possibility she would be able to afford the running costs. The house would probably have to be sold. As the wheels of her car crunched on the long drive, she became irrationally disturbed about meeting Ada Bray and regretted that she had not insisted on the housekeeper leaving the property before her arrival. She longed to have been issued with a key so she could look around privately.

There was ample parking space for multiple cars at the side of the house. Morwenna pulled up the handbrake of her modest Toyota and reluctantly swung her feet on to the scorched ground. Sweat trickled between her shoulder blades and her hands were clammy with fear. She hoped that Harriet was making good progress and would only be a couple of hours behind her. During the later part of the journey, Morwenna had conjured Ada Bray into an embittered spinster, tall and craggy-faced. She would be out to make things difficult for Edith's heir.

As she climbed out of the driving seat, a grey-haired lady appeared from around the back of the house. Ada was plump, short and full of smiles. The complete opposite to what Morwenna expected. She had a soft face, tiny brown eyes and a wide mouth. Beaming from ear to ear, Ada approached the car. She called from a short distance that she wanted to shake hands but she was being cautious due to her age and the need for social distancing. Ada introduced herself by her first name and Morwenna did the same.

It was such a beautiful day that Ada led Morwenna around to the front of the property, which faced the sea and cliffs directly, and invited her to sit at a wrought iron table for afternoon tea. Ada had gone to a considerable amount of trouble to give her visitor a warm welcome. She prepared a cream tea, including clotted cream, home-made strawberry jam and freshly baked fruit scones. The seating area at the front of the property was relatively small compared to the huge size of the house but Morwenna could see that there were very large gardens around the other two sides. In truth, she was itching to explore outside and inside but she felt a little shy to do so even though she was, pending the confirmation of probate, the owner!

With commendable restraint, Morwenna sat still with Ada and observed her immediate surroundings. The garden furniture was a little scuffed and worn but was clearly of high quality. From what she could see, the south facing terrace was in a reasonably tidy state and guarded by sturdy chest-high railings from the cliff edge that fell to the rocks and beach below. She commented on a massive oak tree, its roots pushing up the slabs at the corner of patio and Ada said she thought it may have been there for over a hundred years. Ada made friendly small talk, asking Morwenna about the journey and they both complimented the weather.

'Cornwall always looks so beautiful on sunny days', remarked Ada.

'I've never been to Cornwall, or even Devon', replied Morwenna.

Ada looked surprised by this remark.

'Oh, replied Ada', rather vaguely. 'I thought you might have visited the West Country before'.

'No', said Morwenna. 'My grandparents were born and brought up in Cornwall, and the whole family re-located to Yorkshire before I was born. We took our holidays abroad and occasionally in the Lake District or the Yorkshire Dales. I know very little about my Cornish roots and that's one of the reasons I agreed to attend in person, to deal with my great aunt's estate.'

'Where do you live now?' asked Ada

'I live in Bath with my husband. We tend to take holidays during winter months. My husband's daughters live in Australia, you see,' explained Morwenna.

The housekeeper nodded, but did not offer any views or comments on Morwenna's heritage. Morwenna formed the distinct impression that Ada took her opportunity to change the topic away from family history.

'Ah, I should tell you that the solicitor rang,' said Ada. 'Angela Smalley wants to see you as soon as possible. I suggested she could call at the house tomorrow, rather than you attending the office in Truro and she agreed. The appointment can take place outside.'

'Excellent,' replied Morwenna.

Morwenna was relieved that she would not have to negotiate Truro. Ada offered her a guided tour of the house and garden and Morwenna leapt up. After jumping out of her seat, she tried to cover her eagerness by pausing periodically in the grounds. She feigned a relaxed posture, when the opportunity arose. As a keen amateur historian, she delayed the housekeeper with conversation about architecture. The visitor wondered if the property was Georgian. Ada confirmed that the house was built in about 1810.

Ada explained about the gardener, Joseph Penhaligon, who was now in his late seventies. He only worked a few hours per week and otherwise, he was a recluse. He mowed the lawns and kept the south terrace tidy and clear, but much of the rest of the garden had become considerably overgrown. Joseph suffered from a *condition*, which meant he could only work intermittently, so sometimes he was off work for several weeks or even a couple of months at a time. In any event, he never worked on a Monday or Tuesday, so Morwenna would not meet Joseph until later in the week. She imagined he would not welcome her visiting him without an invitation, if he liked to keep himself to himself.

Morwenna estimated that the garden was around three acres. The south terrace was small and faced directly out to sea from the *front* of the house. The drive entered at the west side of the house, and the larger areas of garden were at the north and east. It was easy to stroll across the lawns but trees and shrubbery had grown up around the perimeter of the garden. The wall surrounding the grounds had therefore become inaccessible. She decided to stay with Ada today and make a thorough exploration at a later time, with more appropriate clothing and footwear. The borders were a tangle of shrubs, trees and clumps of thorned bushes.

Living in a town flat, Morwenna was no gardener but she still had the urge to make a thorough inspection of the grounds. There was various out-buildings, including a rather dilapidated summer house and an overgrown grass tennis court in the back garden to the north of the property. To the south of the property was a steep path and steps down to a small private beach. The beach could otherwise only be reached by water or the sea shore at very low tides. Also, on the east side was a gate leading to a small cottage where Joseph Penhaligon lived. Morwenna did not like to ask if he owned the cottage or whether she was his landlord.

The summer house was padlocked and she elected not to descend the steps to the beach because she was wearing the wrong shoes and she thought it might be a bit steep for Ada. There would be plenty of time to explore later. They entered the house through the back door, at the east of the property. Ada explained that the front door was rarely used nowadays.

The back door led the two women directly into the kitchen, via an overgrown kitchen garden. Morwenna could not pinpoint the date of the kitchen. There were original slate tiles on the floor, oak cupboards, probably Victorian, a range and an ancient comfy sofa. To her surprise, there was a huge, wiry Scottish deerhound asleep, with his nose buried in the rug. The dog slowly lifted his eyelids and casually climbed to his feet. He trotted over at a steady pace, claws clattering on the floor, with his ears pricked-up. He did not bark or jump-up but sniffed at Morwenna's hand and licked it affectionately. She was not really used to dogs so she stepped back cautiously.

'Don't be frightened of Titan', said Ada. 'He's a friendly dog although he has been quite sad since Miss Nancarrow died.'

'So, he hopefully won't bite me?' asked Morwenna warily.

'That's odd,' said Ada. 'He's wagging his tail and greeting you like an old friend. He's usually quite dismissive of humans he has never met before. He tends to ignore strangers.'

Morwenna was surprised that Ada did not use Edith Nancarrow's christian name, but she said nothing. This was the first mention of her great aunt. She did not like to pry so soon and she thought Ada could be quite upset about Edith's death. Although the housekeeper had been extremely friendly and chattered throughout the tour of the garden, she had revealed nothing of any consequence. Morwenna suspected Ada was sizing her up for the time being.

The housekeeper showed her visitor a small room off the kitchen, which had previously been the butler's pantry but was now a private sitting room used by Ada. The interior was quite bleak and gloomy except for two armchairs which were covered in a fresh, bright floral fabric. Wooden shelves boasted the dusty crystal, china and faded table linens of bygone times. There was a tall iron-grey fireplace and a tiny mullioned window overlooking the tangled kitchen garden. Ada opened a narrow door at the far side of the room which revealed steep stone steps leading to the wine cellar.

'There's a few hundred bottles of wine down there,' said Ada pointing down the steps.

Interesting, thought Morwenna, Ada has her own sitting room and called Edith, Miss Nancarrow. Perhaps Ada was treated as an employee rather than companion?

The visitor casually followed Ada from the kitchen into the main hall. The room was impressive with a curved mahogany staircase, as the dominant feature. A stained-glass window, part way up, cast multi-coloured beams of light over the banisters and Morwenna gasped in appreciation. She couldn't maintain her careless veneer now. Several oil paintings hung on the walls and Ada explained that these featured various Nancarrow ancestors.

Ada pointed to an oil portrait of a man and woman, identifying them as Jory and Hedra Nancarrow, Morwenna's great grandparents. The painting depicted the couple in the flush of youth. Hedra was wearing a heavy, luxurious cream brocade evening gown. Her ivory beaded shawl spiralled behind the couple, and onto a Persian rug beneath their feet. Her appearance was lively and untroubled and her fair hair was displayed in a cascade of soft ringlets. In contrast to his wife, Jory was bearded, gaunt and raven-haired. He dressed in a dark suit and he wore a serious but spirited expression. Morwenna thought his angular features were striking, but not handsome. Not a man to be crossed, she imagined.

'It was painted soon after Jory and Hedra's marriage,' said Ada.

Their clothes were Edwardian in style, possibly from the early 1900's. This era was compatible with their birthdates which were around 1880 according to Morwenna's more recent revisions of her family history.

She had now memorised enough of her family tree to know that her grandfather Frank Nancarrow was the son of Jory and Hedra, and Edith Nancarrow was their daughter who had been considerably younger than Frank. For the first time it occurred to Morwenna as very odd that this house, estate and family heirlooms had been inherited by a younger sister in the 1950s, especially at a time when sons were often favoured over daughters. She made a mental note to interrogate the solicitor about that the following day.

Downstairs there was a morning room, cloak room and a study in the south wing of the property and a library, to the west, overlooking Loe Bar Road. The sitting room and dining room faced north. The dining room and sitting room had French windows with a view over the lawned gardens, summer house and tennis court. The hall and each reception room had oak flooring and all the furniture was period Georgian or Victorian. Large but threadbare rugs covered the central part of each room. The rooms were crowded and cluttered but lived-in. It was as if, furniture and ornaments had been added, over the last one hundred years, and nothing ever taken away.

The study and library were packed with papers and books. Edith obviously spent a lot of time in the study as there were two well-worn armchairs by the fireplace. Ada explained that Miss Nancarrow would often sit in the study in the evenings by the fire, before she became too infirm to move up and down the stairs easily. After that she was usually confined to her bedroom. Morwenna hoped that Edith's financial affairs were a bit tidier and more organised than her house. Edith's private possessions, such as her glasses and purse, appeared to have been left where they were.

'How was Edith before she died?' asked Morwenna.

'Her body was becoming weak and she struggled with the stairs, but her brain was very sharp,' said Ada.

'Even right at the end?' enquired Morwenna.

'Oh yes,' replied Ada. 'Even on her last day she was bright and talk-ative. The only thing I would say, about her last few days, was that she was restless. Like she was expecting something and becoming inpatient.'

'Do you think she knew the end was coming?' asked Morwenna.

'She seemed more excited than anything else,' replied Ada without further explanation.

Ada noticed her visitor glancing at Edith's shoes under the chair and her pill box on the mantlepiece.

'I didn't like to move anything at all. It's the risk of being accused of something, you see, so I've not touched any of Miss Nancarrow's possessions,' Ada said with an edge to her voice that Morwenna had not detected before.

'Yes, I understand,' replied Morwenna.

The two women climbed the stairs. There were five large bedrooms and two bathrooms on the first floor. Ada explained that there were various small bedrooms and the nursery on the top floor, used by a small army of servants in days gone by. The housekeeper said that she occupied one bedroom in the old staff quarters. They didn't go up the second flight of steps because Ada explained that the top floor was mainly used for storage nowadays.

The housekeeper introduced each bedroom on the first floor in turn. The master bedroom was found over the sitting room and overlooked the lawned garden to the north. This had obviously belonged to Edith and again, all her personal possessions were in evidence. Her jumble of books and papers extended up here as well. Ada had assigned Morwenna and Harriet the two bedrooms in the south wing of the house which overlooked the sea. Apparently, these were lovely in summer but quite noisy with the crashing waves and high winds during winter. This was why the grander bedrooms were located to the north, overlooking the garden. Morwenna had been allocated the bedroom over the morning room and Harriet the bedroom over the study.

Morwenna had briefly forgotten that her friend was arriving that day. She was looking forward to showing off *Gwedr Iowarth* and she also wanted to share some of her thoughts, which she could not discuss with the housekeeper. Ada announced that she could have dinner ready for seven o'clock and Morwenna said that Harriet should have arrived by then. Morwenna was grateful that they would have dinner prepared for them, although she felt a bit uncomfortable and wasn't sure whether Ada would join them for dinner or not. Maybe she would, *go with the flow* for now and allow the housekeeper to determine any routine until she had a better handle on the situation.

'Just stopping for the loo. Should be there in ½ hour, Harri xx,' Morwenna's mobile phone chirped up a message from Harriet.

'Brace yourself to be amazed, Wenna xx,' she texted back.

Morwenna carried her cases up to her bedroom and gazed out of the window. There was so much she wanted to ask and do that she felt quite overwhelmed and decided to do nothing. She returned outside again and sat on the south terrace and waited for Harriet to arrive. Ada brought her a cup of coffee and retired to the kitchen to make preparations for dinner.

Morwenna looked out over the sea and absorbed the warm sunshine and let thoughts run through her head unchallenged. She started to make a mental note of all the questions she wanted to ask the solicitor. She was much less curious about the financial situation than the family story. How come she had a hundred-year-old great aunt living in the ancestral family home, about whom she knew nothing, until four weeks ago? Why had *all this* been left to Edith Nancarrow, who was a younger female sibling, not the older son when her great grandparents had died in the 1950's and why was it bequeathed to Morwenna now?

'There must be a perfectly *innocent* explanation for all of this,' she whispered to herself, and how wrong she was.

Morwenna was not normally prone to falling asleep in the day but she must have dropped off for a short time, while sitting in the late afternoon sunshine. She awoke from her day-dream with a start, and the sound of a scream was carried on an updraft from the cliffs below. She shook herself awake and realised the cry was in her dream. How odd, she must have been more tired than she thought.

Her thoughts were disturbed by the rumble of her friend's car arriving in the drive. Harriet parked and they embraced briefly before remembering that they were meant to be *social distancing*, because of the pandemic. Harriet had the demeanour of someone who hadn't faced the hardships of life and she found interest and joy in the smallest of things. She was endlessly inquisitive and optimistic.

'Hey, Wenna,' said Harriet. 'Its enormous and fabulous. You can't sell it!'

'Harri, I shall never sell it,' Morwenna confirmed.

After a quick cup of coffee, served by Ada, Morwenna replicated the visit of the garden and house with Harriet. She punctuated the tour with queries about her family history. Harriet did well to curtail her childish impulse to skip around the house with glee. They didn't have long because supper was planned for seven o'clock. By the end of their exploration, both of them seemed to have more questions than answers. To her surprise, Morwenna noted that the dining room was set for two, not three. She knocked on the kitchen door and asked Ada about the dining arrangements and whether she could do anything to help. Ada said she usually put the meal through the hatch between the kitchen and dining room for Miss Nancarrow and the new proprietor agreed to that.

The two visitors tentatively asked Ada to dine with them but this was met by a somewhat perplexed look and Ada said she was more comfortable eating in the kitchen, so Morwenna did not pressure her. They were served beef stew and dumplings for the main course and jam sponge for pudding which they devoured ravenously after a tiring and exciting day. Before they had a chance to carry the plates back through to the kitchen, the housekeeper informed them that she would clear away and she would bring coffee to the study, so they both complied. They were loathed to disrupt Ada's usual routine and it seemed like Edith had usually sat in the study after supper. It would probably difficult to change the traditional rhythms of the house until the old lady left.

The two women were exhausted and, although Harriet was impatient to explore, they agreed that it looked a bit greedy to start poking around, at least until the conversation with the solicitor had taken place the following day. Morwenna needed to be satisfied that the inheritance was rightfully hers. In her usual self-deprecating manner, she worried that her legacy was some bizarre mistake. In any case, Morwenna was not an avaricious person and Harriet did not want to be seen as such!

The mantle clock struck ten and Morwenna looked at Harriet. Her weary head sagged into the wing of the chair and her eyes were closed. Morwenna nudged her arm and suggested they both retire to bed.

Chapter 3

The Will

Breakfast was served in the dining room, via the kitchen-hatch, the following morning. Angela Smalley, the solicitor, was due to arrive soon after nine o'clock. Morwenna invited Harriet to join them for the meeting and she readily agreed. Harriet did not suffer with any pretentions of confidentiality or discretion. Morwenna knew her companion would have surely either eavesdropped or insisted on hearing every last morsel of information later on, had she not been allowed to join them. In any case Morwenna wanted Harriet to know everything so that she could help her navigate through the next few weeks. Harriet, on the other hand, congratulated herself on the self-discipline she had exhibited so far in keeping her questioning of Ada to a minimum and refraining from looking through the desk drawers the previous night.

The two friends were already installed on the south terrace before Angela Smalley arrived. There were two stone bird tables with a bird bath in between. Once Harriet and Morwenna had been motionless for a while, a blackbird started splashing himself in the bird bath and then perched on the edge to dry. He cocked his head at them, self-assured and arrogant. He only flew off, when *he* was ready. The bird was momentarily buffeted by the breeze sweeping up the cliff and then he turned inland and flew into the adjacent oak tree, to observe the proceedings from a distance.

'That bird table is very similar to the one you bought for Edward for his sixtieth birthday,' commented Morwenna. 'It nearly killed us carrying it to the car from the reclamation yard.'

'Thankfully the base was hollow, or I don't think we could have moved it,' reflected Harriet. 'You're right though, the arts and crafts style carvings and thick base are very similar.'

They greeted Angela Smalley with nods rather than hand-shakes due to the rules about social distancing. Angela introduced herself on first-name terms so Morwenna and Harriet did the same. Angela started by checking Morwenna's identity. Angela examined her passport, driving licence, birth and marriage certificates and declared she was satisfied. Once the legal formalities were dealt with, the two women settled down and listened in earnest to what the solicitor had to say.

Edith Nancarrow was over one hundred years old on the date of her death, 29th May 2020. She had been born on 9th January 1920 at *Gwedr Iowarth* and had lived there until the day of her death. She had been in relatively good health for her age and she had been found dead in bed by Ada Bray, who had entered her bedroom at around eight o'clock on 29th May, to help her dress. In her last year she had become increasingly frail and struggled with the stairs and she was 'shielding' at the time of her death to avoid corona virus. Having not seen her GP recently, a post-mortem had been required and the immediate cause of death was a, *cerebrovascular incident* or a stroke in everyday terms.

Edith was a spinster and she had left a will, written in July 1966, leaving everything to Morwenna Catherine Trevethan, her great niece. Harriet pointed out to the solicitor that the will had been written with Morwenna as the sole beneficiary, when she was less than four weeks old. Angela nodded and her expression did not change. Either she already knew why and she had an excellent poker face or maybe she did not know the significance.

Before Morwenna had a chance, Harriet asked, 'Was there any will before that?'

'Erm let me have a look?' said Angela rooting through the file. 'Prior to your birth, the entire estate was left to Helston Children's Home.'

'Blimey,' said Morwenna.

'So, who *could* Edith have left her estate to at that stage?' asked Morwenna.

'In 1966 both your parents were alive, your mother Ebrel Nancarrow was born in 1939 and as you know she died in 2001. Edith's brother, Frank Nancarrow was still alive in 1963. He was born in 1905 and died in 1972. So, yes under normal circumstances I would have expected to find the estate of a spinster left to Edith's brother Frank or her niece Ebrel,' replied Angela, without giving any explanation.

Angela examined the papers again and found an even older will, detailing a *Catherine Nicholas* as the heir, until the will was changed to favour Helston Children's home in February 1963.

'Who is Catherine Nicholas?' asked Morwenna.

'Her full name is Catherine Angela Nicholas', replied the solicitor. 'Catherine's date of birth according to the old will is 24th December 1943 and her address was here. I mean Gwedr Iowarth. Sorry I don't know anything more about her.'

Angela continued, seemingly unperturbed, 'In 1998 Edith Nancarrow purchased a terraced house in Falmouth and created a small trust fund to pass to Ada Bray at the time of Edith's death. Otherwise, her estate is intact.'

Angela provided a verbal summary of Edith's legacy and promised the more extensive portfolio would follow in writing. The documents detailing the entire estate and holdings would need quite a lot of time to absorb. In summary Edith had owned Gwedr Iowarth and Gwedr Iowarth Cottage outright. She had around £250,000 cash in banks and building societies and around £1.2 million in various stocks and shares, with shipping investments comprising about a third.

The approximate value of the house was £1.8 million, although like most properties situated close to Cornwall cliffs, there was always a possible future chance of erosion affecting the value. In some parts of Cornwall, properties were at risk of falling into the sea. Though there was certainly no short, or medium-term risk of this happening to Gwedr Iowarth. According to a recent structural and geological report, the proximity of the property to the cliffs, could affect mortgaging or elevate the costs of insurance. There was also jewellery valued at around £50,000 in the safe.

Morwenna was staggered and she sat back in her chair, eyes uplifted to the sky, looking overwhelmed. She and her husband Jonathan had enough money and a comfortable lifestyle. She retired early on a social services pension and Jonathan had a more than adequate pension from Bradders Bank, where he previously worked. However, this amount of wealth was an outright *game changer,* as Harriet pointed out in her typically undignified manner.

Morwenna thought about the family tree and methodically spoke her thoughts out loud to Angela and Harriet.

'So, Jory and Hedra Nancarrow, who were born in the 1880's lived in the family home, *Gwedr Iowarth.* They had two children, Frank Nancarrow, born in 1905 and his much younger sister Edith Nancarrow, born in 1920. They chose to leave the house and their entire estate to Edith, rather than Frank. Why would they do that?'

'I don't know the background,' said Angela thoughtfully, 'There could be more paperwork in the archives. I only started practicing here over the last few years after my father retired, when he had a stroke. However, he still owns the firm and he may be able to give you some information so I'll get back to you on that.'

Seemingly, Angela had concluded the necessary business with her client for the day. Having imparted the information, she rose decisively to her feet.

'Shall I contact Morgan-Fletcher estate agents to market the house?' asked Angela crisply, as she walked away from the table.

'No, no, absolutely not,' said Morwenna firmly. 'There is quite a lot we need to get to the bottom of, before I decide what to do next.'

'Oh, I nearly forgot,' said Angela impassively. 'Here is the key for the safe. It's behind the picture of a ship in the study. I'll call you tomorrow and arrange to meet up, with further information. Let's see if I can answer any of your queries.'

With that, Angela blipped her car, jumped inside and drove away. For a few minutes, the two friends sat in silence. They were too astonished to speak.

'Well let's go and have a look in the safe, shall we?' said Harriet, who couldn't contain her eagerness to start examining the inheritance.

Morwenna felt bolder and even quite intrepid, now that she was sure the house belonged to her. Earlier she had been tempted to ask for permission at every move, and even now, she felt irrationally guilty at the prospect of walking into the study and searching through the safe.

'Come on then,' urged Harriet. She was typically undaunted by the whole business.

They exited the south terrace and re-entered the house through the front door. This was the first time they had gone in that way, after Morwenna had worked out how to unlock it from the inside. Entering by the front door allowed them to access the study and other rooms off the main hall without being observed by Ada, who was usually in the kitchen.

Morwenna and Harriet scrutinised the study. The room was dominated by a large wooden desk, opposite the window and the walls were lined with book shelves. There were two comfy armchairs by the fire place. Harriet picked up the spectacles from the desk and proclaimed that Edith must have been significantly long sighted like most older people. She folded the glasses and placed them in the top drawer of the desk where they could not be seen. Harriet did not like to see Edith's possessions lying around as if she was still alive. It felt dishonourable somehow.

Harriet scanned the walls of the study which looked gloomy compared with the brilliant sunshine on the terrace. She quickly located the safe behind a large, agreeable oil painting of a non-specific sailing ship. Together, they lifted the picture off its hook and placed the key in the lock which had obviously been in regular use and opened quite easily with a satisfying oily click. Inside they found the deeds to *Gwedr Iowarth*, several velvet and leather boxes and a very large pile of, *page to a day*, diaries dating from 1935 to 1963, although on closer inspection, the years from World War 2 were missing.

The two women sat down at the desk and started to look through the boxes. The jewel cases had sumptuous velvet cushions. There was a large diamond ring, a solid gold Cartier watch and a magnificent ruby necklace. Morwenna inspected the gold lockets containing portraits of long-passed friends and relatives. Harriet, being Harriet, adorned herself in the jewellery as it was lifted out. Unfortunately, Ada walked in while Harriet was modelling her regalia and they all felt slightly embarrassed. Harriet even felt herself blush, although Ada did not register any sign of displeasure. The housekeeper explained that Miss Nancarrow, as she always called Edith, had worn the diamond ring daily but the rest had not been worn for many years.

'Yes, the diamond ring was on Miss Nancarrow's finger when she died,' explained Ada primly. 'The undertaker wanted to give it to me for safe-keeping. I didn't let him, of course. I made him take the ring to the solicitor who put it in the safe when she visited here to make the arrangements for the funeral.'

Morwenna was curious about many things and she was aware that Ada had worked at *Gwedr Iowarth* for years. She now felt sufficiently adventurous to start trying to extract a few details.

'You must have seen a lot of changes in this house while you have worked here, Ada?' asked Morwenna using her typical diplomacy.

'Oh yes,' Ada replied, 'I first came here as a maid in the spring of 1962, when I was only fifteen.'

'How old are you now?' asked Harriet bluntly.

'I'm seventy-three and ready to retire!' replied Ada, laughing at Harriet's outspokenness.

'Where were you before?' asked Morwenna, even though she knew some of Ada's history. She was curious to see what the housekeeper would divulge.

'I was living in Helston Children's Home. I had nowhere to go before Miss Nancarrow took me in and gave me a job. I'm sure Miss Smalley told you that she has also provided for my retirement.'

'Yes, she has, of course,' answered Morwenna.

At first Morwenna thought Ada would open up and tell her a lot more but she quickly re-directed the conversation.

'Anyway,' said Ada, 'I'm just checking that you are OK for an early lunch, maybe twelve o'clock and I'll leave you a buffet for your supper. It's my afternoon and evening off, and I normally go to my amateur-dramatics rehearsal in the evening but that's on hold for now because of the pandemic. I will need to visit Falmouth this afternoon, though. Is that all right?'

'Golly, yes,' said Morwenna. 'Have you a lot to do?'

'I've given notice to the tenants in my house in Falmouth and I need to visit the letting agent to make arrangements for my move. I'm hoping to be in by August at the latest, maybe before, if that's all right with you'.

'Yes, absolutely fine,' replied Morwenna.

'Will you be back this evening?' asked Morwenna, half hoping she would be out all night.

'Yes, I'll be back at about eight. Could you take Titan for a walk while I'm out and give him his dinner later on?' requested Ada.

'No problem,' answered Morwenna.

Directly after lunch the housekeeper walked into Porthleven to take the bus to Falmouth, leaving the two friends alone in the house for the first time. Morwenna could tell by Ada's manner that she was still on her guard. When the older woman left the house, Morwenna felt lighter and unshackled. She was prompted by a sense of urgency, to discover the secrets of Gwedr Iowarth.

'OK,' said Morwenna. 'Let's write our queries down and then walk the dog, to clear our minds.'

'What are the *main* questions?' asked Harriet.

'Why did Jory and Hedra Nancarrow leave their estate and money to their younger daughter, Edith? asked Morwenna.

'Surely in those days,' replied Harriet, 'everything should have been left to the oldest son Frank?'

'Secondly, why did Edith not include my mother and grandfather in her earlier wills? Oddly, as soon as I was born, she changed her will leaving everything to me.' observed Morwenna. 'She never even met me!'

'Also why did Edith previously bequeath everything to a children's home and before that, to Catherine Nicholas and who is Catherine Nicholas?' demanded Harriet.

'Most importantly, why didn't my parents and grandparents tell me anything about this?' concluded Morwenna.

Together, they jotted down each question on paper and this marked the start of their investigation. Presently they proceeded to the kitchen to collect Titan. His lead was hanging by the back door and he bounded over as soon as Morwenna lifted it off the hook. Titan was aptly named. He was tall, even for a Scottish deerhound, and wore a coat of coarse blue-grey fur which was at the darker end of the spectrum for his breed. He had rather sad eyes and Morwenna thought he must be missing Edith. She wondered how old he was and what should be done with him in future. Jonathan did not like dogs and Titan would be far too big for their flat in Bath.

The two women wore walking shoes so they could descend the path safely to the beach. Although the steps were steep, they were fairly well maintained and Titan was obviously used to them. Due to his large size, he lolloped down the steps in an ungainly manner. It was a bit cooler and windier than the previous day but the views were stunning. Toothed ridges of cloud fenestrated the sky, allowing the sun to throw silver beams of light onto the waves. Once they climbed over the rocks and pools, Morwenna and Harriet arrived on the sandy part of the beach. Titan strained on his lead, so he was released and went charging across the beach. Harriet commented on the speed of Titan's run. She suggested he was a young dog and her friend nodded in agreement.

Morwenna looked behind her at the cliff which had a sheer forty-foot drop from the fenced south terrace of the house, to the rocks and rock pools below. Harriet hated heights and she also had a morbid fear of water and drowning. It took a bit of persuasion for her to follow Morwenna around the shoreline which would be submerged when the tide came in. The sea was a long way out, so they were able to walk around the foot of the cliffs, to access the public beach in the next inlet. Titan tore after them each time they edged away from him. He was obviously very well trained because he came back willingly, to be put on his lead, as they arrived at the gate between the public beach and the adjacent road.

From the crowded beach, they walked into the outskirts of Porthleven planning to return home via the road. Harriet suggested they should not risk re-tracing their steps, as they would be cut-off by the tide which was now coming in. Morwenna was sure they could have made it back safely via the beach but Harriet refused. She was not frightened of many things but her friend knew water and heights were something that was non-negotiable.

They walked and chatted companionably, making an action plan as they went.

'Let's start by researching Catherine Nicholas and Helston Children's Home,' said Harriet.

'You're right,' replied Morwenna, 'There are two connections with the children's home. Firstly, Ada came from Helston Children's Home when she was fifteen and Edith left the estate to the same home after Catherine Nicholas was taken out of the will.'

'We can search the internet, to see if we can find anything out about Catherine Nicholas,' suggested Harriet. 'We might be able to contact Catherine?'

Both women were out of shape and struggled to keep up with the dog on the steep incline up to the house. Morwenna passed the lead to Harriet and Titan helped pull her up the hill, such was his strength and enthusiasm. Morwenna stopped walking and leant against a lamp post and Harriet had to sit down for a few minutes on a bench, as she was still struggling to catch her breath. Her legs felt wobbly and unruly. She stamped her feet on the ground to relieve the pins and needles in her toes. Once Harriet was moving again, her legs were better behaved although they were still aching with fatigue.

At last, they came to the brow of the hill and, by then, even Titan was glad to catch a glimpse of Gwedr Iowarth in the distance. Morwenna gazed at the tranquil beauty of her new home, set in the lush green mantle of summer. The wind had dropped and there was a vague afternoon haze causing the contour of the house to shiver and flex in the westerly sun. She experienced a sense of awe she had not experienced in months or even years.

Chapter 4

The Start of the Investigation

Morwenna and Harriet re-entered the house through the kitchen door after their walk with Titan. He drank enthusiastically from his bowl and then he nudged the dish towards Morwenna's feet for her to re-fill it, which she did. Next, they headed for the library. The dog followed them, bumping the swell of his haunch against Morwenna's thigh, as she strolled along. The tip of his tail whipped against her calf causing a novel, yet comforting stinging sensation. They cleared the large table in the library to use as a base for their investigations. Titan settled himself down, close to his new favourite human's feet. Morwenna opted to use her laptop to find out about Catherine Nicholas, through her genealogy website and Harriet chose to conduct some research about Helston Children's Home.

Morwenna had become experienced in the use of her genealogy website. She typed in the name, *Catherine Angela Nicholas* and date of birth as provided by the solicitor, 24th December 1943. It occurred to her that Catherine was a so called, *war baby*. She had no idea where she was born but took a guess at her being connected with Cornwall and Porthleven, so entered these details in the search engine. She quickly established that Catherine was dead and she had died in the first quarter of 1963 (January to March 1963). Otherwise, there was very little information about her. Morwenna clicked through to order her death certificate, and opted to pay extra to have it e-mailed to her. When she selected the birth certificate, an advisory note popped up which she had never seen before. She was informed that a *foundling registrar certificate* was available, but not a birth certificate, so she ordered that instead. The place of birth was unknown, but the registrar had recorded Helston as the location where she was discovered.

'Harri,' Morwenna shouted, leaping to her feet and causing poor Titan to jump out of his skin, 'Catherine was a foundling. You know, a baby who was abandoned.'

Titan looked inquisitively at Harriet and his mistress and then settled himself down again and shut his eyes. This time he sat on Morwenna's feet, which stopped her from pacing around the room in excitement. Harriet was similarly intrigued by their newest discovery.

'Ok, so maybe Edith disliked your mother and grandfather so much, she left everything to a foundling?' speculated Harriet.

'There's got to be more to it than a family argument,' replied Morwenna. 'Also, Catherine died really young. She was only twenty.'

'We certainly *won't* be contacting her for more information,' said Harriet, somewhat heartlessly.

Harriet had discovered that the children's home in Helston had opened as, *Helston Home for Boys* in 1901. The institution had started taking girls in 1919, after the First World War, and the home had finally closed in 1985. Edith Nancarrow joined the Board of Governors in 1945 and then became Chair of the Governors. She remained so until the establishment closed.

'Bingo,' shouted Harriet a few minutes later, as she described the contents of an article published in *The Cornish News Chronicle* on 29th December 1943: *A new-born baby girl was left in the entrance hall of Helston Children's home some time after 9 PM on 24th December 1943. There are no clues to the identity of the child. She has been named Catherine after the home's cook, who found her as she was leaving the building, at the end of her shift.'* The paper recorded that the other children had suggested a middle name of Angela (after the Christmas angel) and the vicar had suggested Nicholas after St Nicholas, considering the time of year. A subsequent article the following week, informed by the local police, detailed no leads in discovering the child's real identity. The story then disappeared from the news, as the papers were largely dedicated to the war effort and the battle of Monte Cassino where a number of troops from Helston had lost their lives.

'OK, so Catherine Nicholas was a foundling,' summarised Morwenna, 'and she was left as a new-born in the entrance of Helston Children's Home on Christmas Eve 1943. Her identity was presumably never found. After the war, Edith became associated with the establishment as a governor. Maybe she became fond of Catherine and brought her to live with her here, perhaps as a foster child or companion? We know from the solicitor that Catherine was living at *Gwedr Iowarth* at the time of her death in early 1963, when she would have been only just twenty years old.'

'Surely Ada must be able to help us shed some light on this,' said Harriet. 'She came here in 1962 and she was from the same children's home.'

'That's true,' replied Morwenna, 'but let's hold back a little. We don't want Ada to know about our little investigation just yet. She seems quite guarded at the moment and I don't want her to think we are being too nosey for the time being.'

'What makes you say that?' said her companion.

'Have you noticed? If you ask her anything about the past. She tells you a little bit, details she knows we already have. Then she changes the subject,' explained Morwenna.

Harriet was frustrated at her friend's reluctance to interrogate the housekeeper, but she agreed to remain discrete, for now anyway.

'Blimey,' said Morwenna, 'It's late. We need to think about making some supper and feeding Titan.'

Titan was still sitting, loyally, on Morwenna's feet, making them quite numb but he jumped up with the apparent mention of food. He beat his tail against the chair in anticipation of dinner. They made their way into the kitchen and decided to eat at the kitchen table rather than carry food into the dining room. Harriet took the buffet out of the fridge and Morwenna opened a large tin of dog food for Titan, which he wolfed down. Harriet un-corked a bottle of chilled white wine and they enjoyed the salad and cold meats left for them by Ada.

After supper Harriet was exhausted. Her post-viral symptoms still lingered and she was forced to go to bed very early. Morwenna moved into the study to wait for Jonathan to call, closely followed by Titan, her shadow. In fact, she noticed that Titan clung to her side but he was rather indifferent to Harriet. At around eight o'clock, she heard Ada return and the dog made no move to go and welcome her, remaining closely by his Morwenna's feet.

At that moment, the house phone rang and Morwenna snatched it up. Jonathan tended to call her at about 8.30 pm in the UK, from Sydney where it was 7.30 am. She had last spoken to him before leaving the flat in Bath, when he was still intent on her either not travelling to Cornwall, or at least staying for as shorter time as possible. He stated he was worried about her health and the possibility of catching corona virus. He kept reminding Morwenna of Harriet's quite serious complications having caught the virus, but she had been undeterred. Morwenna was concerned that her husband had become unnecessarily pre-occupied with all her current endeavours.

'Hi, how are you, Jon?' she asked.

'I'm fine darling,' he replied. His voice was muffled and difficult to make out due to the echo on the line.

Morwenna explained about the house and money. Jonathan was suitably surprised by the size of the estate but cautioned his wife against digging up too much of the family history, particularly as it sounded like there had been some sort of falling out between the two branches of the family. He thought that she should wind things up as quickly as possible in Cornwall and probably avoid herself a lot of upset in the process. Because of Jonathan's obvious reluctance about her exploits in Cornwall, she decided to humour him and said she would deal with the financial business as quickly as possible, so that she and Harriet could enjoy a seaside holiday before the property was sold. Titan let out a quiet woof, which Jonathan thankfully didn't hear. Acquiring a large dog in addition to a prospective house move couldn't be mentioned just yet.

Morwenna thought there was no point in sharing too many details and worrying him further. After enquiring after his daughters and grand-children in Australia, she agreed to call in a few days. She instructed him to phone on her mobile phone next time, as she and Harriet may not stay at the house too long. They may decide to tour around Cornwall, now the corona virus restrictions were starting to lift. This was a lie, of course, but Morwenna wanted to keep him from nagging her. It would also avoid her having to think up too many untruths to explain her continued investigations about the house and family history behind it.

'Actually, it's going to be difficult for us to talk at all, for the next couple of weeks,' said Jonathan.

'Why?' asked Morwenna.

'I'm going on an outback trek with Tim,' he replied. 'We thought it was the ideal opportunity. It's something I've always wanted to do and now is the perfect time as I'm stuck here. Anyway, Tim says you can't get a mobile signal for days sometimes.'

'Blimey,' said Morwenna. 'Please be careful. Love you'.

Morwenna was surprised that Jonathan had decided to take a trip with Tim, his son in law. Her husband was seventy-six and she hoped he was *up to it*. However, she did recall Tim describing a similar adventure to Jonathan a few years ago. He had appeared really keen at the time, but he hadn't wanted to leave his new wife alone. She would never have dreamed of undertaking such an expedition herself.

Morwenna began to shiver as the evening became chilly. She lit the electric fire and settled back to deliberate about the current conflict in her marriage. In spite of her troubled thoughts, she quickly dropped off to sleep in the armchair. She glimpsed the winter gardens of *Gwedr Iowarth* in her dreams. A cluster of desperate young people were hurrying through the grounds, disturbing the snow with their boots There was a familiar young man crying, *Cathy*. His appearance transfigured into Jonathan's and a young Ada was rushing towards the house, with tears cascading down her face.

Morwenna awoke with a start. Her heart was thudding and Titan had his paw on her knee. The dog gazed at her with concern and she urged herself to settle down. The name *Gwedr Iowarth* was repeating over and over in her head. The nightmare had been terrifying and palpable. Maybe the contents of the strange dream were due to her guilt about misleading Jonathan. She reached for her laptop to discover what *Gwedr Iowarth* meant in Cornish. The direct translation was *garden mirror*. How odd, thought Morwenna. She would definitely ask Ada about that the next morning.

She arose from her seat and headed towards the stairs. She was followed by Titan who settled himself at the bottom of the stairs on a thick rug which looked just the right size for him. He placed his head on the bottom step and shut his eyes. He looked contented.

Chapter 5

The Mirrors

The next morning both women slept in. It was well after eight o clock by the time they were up and dressed. Morwenna was the first to climb down the stairs, only to bump straight into Titan with his nose still resting on the bottom step. He wagged his tail conscientiously and followed her down the hall. Ada was walking past and bid Morwenna good morning.

'Well Titan has made a real strong bond with you,' Ada said in her noticeable Cornish accent.

'What do you mean?' asked Morwenna.

'It's like you have replaced Miss Nancarrow. He follows you around, as if you were her and he waits for you on his rug at the bottom of the stairs all night. He hasn't done that since his last mistress died. I guess he's your dog now.'

'Oh blimey,' said Morwenna.

'I thought *you* might be taking him to your house in Falmouth?' pleaded Morwenna, 'when you move in August.'

'Gracious no,' said Ada. 'He doesn't really like me and my new cottage will be far too small for such a large dog!'

'How old is Titan?' asked Morwenna.

'He's just turned four,' replied Ada.

'Oh, my goodness,' thought Morwenna. 'What on earth was Jonathan going to say about this?'

Apparently, Titan was the latest in a long line of Scottish deerhounds to live at *Gwedr Iowarth*. His ancestors dated back to the 1880s when Jory and Hedra Nancarrow had resided there. Harriet had joined them by now and she had overheard the conversation about Titan. She pointed to several of the paintings in the hall which featured some of Titan's ancestors. They all wore the same dark grey-blue coarse fur and most of them were bigger than the average deerhound.

'All the dogs have had lovely natures, except that one,' Ada jabbed her stubby finger towards a deerhound who looked very similar to Titan. 'She was called Athena. We thought she was fine, but she once bit your grandmother, Mavis, rather badly on the leg.'

'Oh dear,' replied Morwenna. 'Did you have her put down?'

'No, she was never aggressive again. In fact, her line led to Titan,' Ada replied. 'Miss Nancarrow said she would have to go if it ever happened again, but it didn't.'

Morwenna and Harriet sat down to breakfast. Morwenna explained about her strange dream after Jonathan's phone call. Harriet agreed that her friend was probably suffering from a guilty conscience after lying to Jonathan, on top of too much white wine over supper. However, Harriet was more intrigued by the translation of *Gwedr Iowarth* so they decided to ask Ada for clarification. Ada confirmed that *Gwedr Iowarth* was Cornish for, *The Mirrored Garden.*

'But why is it called that?' asked Harriet.

'Joseph is around today,' Ada replied. 'He'll show you.'

Ada came through to the dining room to clear the breakfast plates while the two women were still drinking their tea, and she started to chatter about her house in Falmouth. She explained that the tenants were moving out at the end of the week and she would decorate and then furnish the house for herself, once they had left. She reminded them that she was happy to remain at *Gwedr Iowarth* while she was needed, but she wanted to be settled in Falmouth by August at the latest. Morwenna should not hesitate to tell Ada if she wanted her to leave sooner. Morwenna encouraged Ada to take any furniture from her sitting room or her bedroom that she wanted and expressed the opinion that Gwedr Iowarth contained far too much furniture. Ada would be doing her a favour to take some of it with her.

'Very kind of you, Morwenna,' Ada replied. 'I will do that. I'm quite attached to some of my furniture. It will be something familiar when I move.'

While Morwenna was coaxing Ada to stay as long as possible, the telephone rang in the hall and Harriet picked it up. It was Angela Smalley asking for Morwenna.

Harriet walked back into the dining room and announced with sarcastic grandiosity, 'Mrs Coutts, the lady of the house. Miss Smalley on the phone for you.'

Morwenna proceeded to the phone and Harriet and Ada remained in the dining room. The housekeeper stopped collecting the plates, as if shocked into stillness. First, she looked startled and next a vexed expression cast across her face. Her normally doughy features became unfamiliarly taut, for a moment. Ada quickly regained her composure and continued her chores.

'I thought Morwenna's surname was Trevethan?' said Ada casually, after a few minutes. Her temperate demeanour had returned.

'Yes, that was her maiden-name, but her married name is *Coutts,*' replied Harriet.

Harriet supposed Ada's transient change in manner had been due to her calling Morwenna, *the lady of the house*. Harriet privately conceded that she had been a bit insensitive, considering Edith had only been dead a few weeks. She kicked herself for being so rude. Firstly, Harriet had been 'caught' wearing the family jewels and now this had probably caused further resentment. She vowed to be more diplomatic in future and slunk out of the room rather sheepishly. Harriet made her way to the kitchen to change into her outdoor shoes as she and Morwenna were going to spend some time exploring the garden.

Morwenna was only on the phone for a few minutes and she told Harriet that Angela Smalley was going to make a further house call to update her, at around four o'clock. She had promised to bring the old family files and some news from her father about why the estate had been left to Edith rather than Morwenna's grandfather, Frank Nancarrow.

Morwenna and Harriet left the house via the kitchen with Morwenna's shadow, Titan, trotting behind her. They walked through the kitchen garden and around the east side of the house, passing the tennis courts and summer house into the main garden to the north of *Gwedr Iowarth*. They immediately spotted Joseph Penhaligon wheeling the lawn mower out of a shed between the tennis court and the summer house. He was older than Morwenna had imagined and she felt quite concerned for his health.

'Hi, Mr Penhaligon. I'm Morwenna and this is my good friend Harriet.'

'Pleased to meet you,' he replied returning Morwenna's smile. 'Call me Joseph.'

Joseph studied Morwenna intently for a few moments and then transferred his gaze to Titan. Unexpectedly tears welled in his eyes and his smile faltered.

'Oh, my goodness, what is the matter?' asked Morwenna, jumping to the conclusion that she had done something out of turn.

'You look just like her, standing there fifty years ago!'

'Who?' interjected Morwenna.

'Miss Nancarrow of course. Actually, it's not just your appearance, although you do look like her. It's the way you stand, your mannerisms, your voice. It's quite uncanny. He can see it too,' Joseph nodded at Titan.

Joseph regained his composure and told the two women he was going to mow the lawns which had been growing vigorously after the warm weather alternating with some night-time rainstorms.

'Can I help you two with anything?' asked Joseph.

'Yes,' replied Morwenna. 'Where can we find the mirrors?'

Joseph pointed at the perimeter walls to the west, north and east of the garden.

'Each wall has a mirror about every ten yards,' he said. 'They are all covered by shrubs nowadays, so you can't see them.'

'What are the mirrors for?' asked Harriet.

'I think they were there to give an illusion of a mysterious *hidden* garden,' Joseph replied. 'Just a Victorian folly for the wealthy, I guess. They had nothing better to do than daydream while the servants did all the work!'

'Where do you think we should start?' asked Morwenna. 'I want to clear one.'

'I think there is a mirror on the wall about six feet to the west of the summer house. I've kept things clearer there than the rest of the garden. That's probably the best place to start. The tools are in the shed,' Joseph laughed and walked off to get on with his mowing.

Once Morwenna saw the power of Joseph's stride, she was less worried about his fitness than she was about her own and Harriet's. Because he had been described as a recluse, she had expected to find the gardener shy or reticent and yet his manner appeared warm. Next time she spoke to Joseph, she would ask him about his age and what his intentions were in respect of the cottage and his work.

The two friends ambled towards the shed hoping for power tools. They were disappointed. Other than the petrol lawn mower, which Joseph had already taken, there was only a selection of ancient hand tools. Morwenna selected a hack saw and Harriet found an old pair of sheers. However, the tools had been kept clean and sharp, so they set to work, after donning lady's gardening gloves they had found on a dusty shelf. They estimated six feet from the summer house and started to remove the shrubbery and tangled weeds in front of the old wall. After about an hour, Harriet had to run inside for refreshments and they both had a little rest. Titan trotted inside with Harriet to drink from his bowl but came straight out again. Morwenna started working once more, while Harriet paused a little longer.

'Stone, I've hit stone,' Morwenna shouted, soon after she re-started.

Harriet leapt up from the lawn and started to feel to the right and left of the wall until her fingertips sensed something smooth. Joseph hadn't been far wrong. Harriet detected one of the mirrors a few inches to the left of where Joseph had told them to search. They both set to work pulling back ivy and clematis until the outline of the mirror was fully revealed. It was shaped like a gothic arch, about five feet high and two feet wide with lead beading dividing it into several panels. There was years of moss and lichen on the surface so they couldn't see anything through it.

This time, Morwenna ran to the kitchen to fetch a bucket of hot soapy water, so they could clean the surface. Harriet took the cloth and started to wipe away layers of grime and Morwenna stood back to watch, with her hands on her hips. Titan was running around in circles and barking with excitement. Harriet's body blocked the mirror until she had finished cleaning it and then she stood to the side for her companion and Titan to admire her handy-work.

'Blimey,' said Morwenna. 'It's like looking into another world. Look, there's a girl in a white cloak….'

Morwenna's attention was fixed on the mirror and her eyes became focussed in the distance. Then she became pale, glanced behind her and fainted.

'Morwenna,' Harriet screamed.

Harriet was hopeless as a doctor when her friends or relatives were unwell and she tended to panic just like anyone else. Joseph was disturbed by Harriet's screams and Titan's frantic barking and he ran over to the two women. Titan was licking Morwenna's face and they knelt over her while she gradually regained consciousness. Joseph went to fetch Ada, who came out with ice wrapped in a towel. They helped her to the garden bench, in a shady spot, in front of the sitting room.

'Sun stroke,' cried Ada. 'I knew you two were doing too much. You're not used to it!'

'Miss Nancarrow was always frightened of those mirrors. She saw a ghost through one, as a child,' said Joseph.

Ada gave Joseph a disparaging look and insisted on putting the ice behind Morwenna's neck. She moved both women in to the sitting room, via the French windows, and she suggested they rest there until lunch. The sitting room, Ada explained, was north facing and it was one of the coolest rooms in the house. Titan looked more shaken than Morwenna and he settled himself down at her feet and eyed her watchfully.

Harriet didn't like to tell Joseph and Ada that it took *almost nothing* to make Morwenna faint but she was concerned about her seeing the girl in a white cloak. Hallucinating wasn't something she usually did! Once they were alone in the sitting room, Harriet quizzed Morwenna about what had happened.

'When you were cleaning the mirror, I couldn't see anything at all. Then you moved to the side and I looked straight into the mirror,' said Morwenna. 'I had the strangest feeling. The reflection was calling me nearer and nearer. It was hard to resist.'

'Then what?' asked Harriet, wondering if she remembered the girl.

'I saw a girl. Well, a woman really because she was tall,' replied Morwenna.

'OK,' said Harriet. 'Any other details?'

'The scene wasn't fully formed. It was vague, but definitely winter. It was snowing and the woman was wearing a white fur cloak and her jet-black hair stood out against the hood of the cloak. Her face was hidden as she was standing sideways. Because I was looking in a mirror, I presumed she was behind me so I turned around to look at her. Then everything went black.'

'That's when you fainted, I suppose,' said Harriet.

'What do you think is wrong with me, Harri?' asked Morwenna. 'First the strange dreams and now this!'

'I think you're just over-tired and Ada's probably right. You have a touch of heat stroke,' Harriet said brightly, although she privately wondered if Morwenna was under more strain than she was letting on. Perhaps her unconscious mind was connecting with the secrets which haunted the house, Harriet thought to herself. Morwenna had always been a spiritual person, in tune with people and objects around her and their history.

'This afternoon, I think I'll have a few hours rest before Angela Smalley comes at four o'clock,' suggested Morwenna.

'That's a good idea,' agreed Harriet.

So, after lunch, Morwenna went to bed and Titan assumed his normal vigil, on the rug at the bottom of the stairs. While her friend was sleeping, Harriet slipped outside to take a second look at the mirror and do a bit more poking around on her own. First of all, she tried to follow the wall around the east, north and west of the garden. There was no wall to the south of the house because the terrace was edged by stout railings, beyond which the cliff plummeted to the beach below.

Joseph Penhaligon had been right. It was impossible for Harriet to move close to the perimeter wall due to accumulated weeds, shrubs and bushes. The only place where she could view the wall directly, was where she and Morwenna had cleared the undergrowth that morning. Ada had explained to them, over lunch, that each mirror was a different shape and size. Years ago, there had been plenty of servants and gardeners, so all the mirrors were kept exposed and polished for the family's amusement.

Harriet made her way back to the arched mirror and placed herself firmly in front of it and stared. If Morwenna can see visions in it, so can I, she thought. She stood there for about fifteen minutes and saw nothing until she really did see Joseph Penhaligon behind her. He had returned from his lunch and he was curious to see what was going on.

'What are you doing?' he smirked.

'Well, Morwenna thought she saw a woman through the mirror. Like a vision,' said Harriet. 'So I decided to come back to ascertain if I could see anything.'

'Did you?' he asked.

'Nope,' said Harriet.

Harriet decided to take this opportunity to question Joseph, but she tried to keep things as casual as possible.

'How long have you been here Joseph?' she asked.

'Most of my life. My dad was head gardener, William Penhaligon, so I was born in *Gwedr Iowarth Cottage*. Do you think she'll throw me out?' he said, referring to Morwenna.

'God no,' Harriet re-assured him. 'Morwenna is the kindest person. I'm sure she'll let you stay.'

'How old are you, if you don't mind me asking?' enquired Harriet.

'War baby. I was born in 1942. I'm seventy-eight.'

'Blimey, you should be retired,' said Harriet.

'I wouldn't know what to do with myself,' Joseph replied. 'This is all I know and gardening helps when I have my episodes.'

'What episodes?' asked Harriet.

'I thought Ada would have told you,' Joseph replied. 'I have schizophrenia. Tablets are really good nowadays though, so that keeps my demons away most of the time. Thank goodness!'

Joseph obviously thought he had said enough, so he told Harriet he needed to go back to work.

'Got to finish the weeding the south terrace,' he shouted as he went. He was a man of few words but Harriet liked him.

Harriet returned to wake Morwenna for the meeting with Angela Smalley. She hoped her friend wouldn't be cross with her for interrogating Joseph.

Chapter 6

Family History

Angela Smalley arrived at four o'clock as planned. They sat on the south terrace again and both Harriet and Morwenna looked expectantly at the solicitor.

'I've spoken to my father,' said Angela. 'It's difficult though, because of his stroke.'

'I'm sorry to have put you to so much trouble,' cut in Morwenna, feeling responsible.

'No don't be,' said Angela. 'It's been quite an interesting tale to try and put together. I gleaned some information from my father and a little bit from the company files.'

Angela explained that her father had inherited the legal business from his father. However, her father had been in university until 1965, so he was reliant on what his father had told him about the Nancarrow family. They also had access to old documents in the firm's archives. Angela had managed to piece together that Jory Nancarrow owned a shipping company in the late 1890s. He had married Hedra in 1904 and Frank Nancarrow, their son, was born in 1905. In his younger days, in the early 1930s, Frank worked for the company as a director. He ran up gambling debts without his father's knowledge which had damaged the company's finances and reputation. Jory had come out of retirement, removed Frank from his position and got the company back on its feet. From that time onwards Jory kept Frank at arms-length from the business. Frank wanted to set up his own enterprise in car manufacturing, so Jory agreed to give him the start-up costs in lieu of his inheritance and the will was changed in favour of Edith, who was only a small child at the time.

Frank and his wife Mavis moved to Leeds in the 1930s. The car manufacturing part of the business was failing but the onset of the second world war, increased demand for engine parts and so a minor part of the business survived. This provided a small income for Frank and Mavis and their daughter Ebrel, who was born in 1939. Letters from Frank, to his father Jory, written in the late 1940s remained in the Kendal-Smalley files. The documents indicated that Frank begged his father to re-write his will but this never happened. Jory died in 1956 leaving everything to Edith.

'I guess Jory was right,' interjected Morwenna. 'From what we know about Frank, everything would have been lost if he had inherited the house and business.'

'Gosh,' said Harriet. 'Jory obviously never forgave Frank.'

'I don't think it was about forgiveness,' interjected Angela Smalley. 'It was about survival. In those days values and reputation were everything. Also, there was no welfare state to fall back on. I think Jory was safe-guarding the survival of the company, the ancestral home and providing a safety net for the extended family. Edith continued to send regular payments to Frank and Mavis to subsidise their lifestyle until 1962.'

'What happened then?' asked Harriet.

'Let me have a look?' said Angela picking up a buff ledger. 'The last monthly payment was made in December 1962.'

'Why did the payments stop?' asked Morwenna.

'It doesn't say,' replied Angela, 'but perhaps things were going better for Frank and his family by then?'

'What happened to *Nancarrow Shipping*?' enquired Harriet.

'Well, that's the clever bit. Edith ran the company successfully until 1972 and then sold it to a Dutch firm, at a very good price, when she retired. She then invested in the Dutch shipping trade and other shipping company shares which was what she knew best and her investments proved very lucrative,' replied Angela.

'Did you ever meet Edith?' Morwenna asked Angela.

'No, not in person,' said Angela. 'She did everything over the phone or documents were posted if anything needed signing. I spoke to her a few times. I did visit the house after she died, to put her ring in the safe.'

Angela rose from her chair and passed copies of the documents she had found across to Morwenna.

'I'll let you know when probate comes through, which should be in the next few days,' said Angela and she left.

As the car drew away, there were ominous rumbles from the north. A few small spots of rain started to splash on the ground and make tiny ripples in the bird bath. The rainfall was gentle for a few seconds but soon it lashed down, hard and fast. Morwenna and Harriet grabbed their paperwork, in a flash of activity, and hastened inside with Titan, who was whining loudly because he didn't like thunder.

They headed for the library, where they were using the big table to spread out the 'evidence', as Harriet called it. Together they looked through the copies of documents Angela Smalley had provided. There was no further factual information to be gleaned from the documents, however both women were keen to examine the photocopy of the letter her Frank wrote to Jory:

5th March 1947

Dearest Papa,

Thank you for your latest cheque which was received with thanks. The small profit we were able to make during the war has disappeared since there is much less demand for engine and car parts with petrol rationing and no contracts from the Ministry of Defence. We rely almost entirely on your allowance to survive. To be honest, I am worried that when you are no longer here, Edith won't have the same commitment to me, Mavis and Ebrel.

Perhaps you will re-consider the will, now that I am settled and my more reckless youthful mistakes are behind me.

Your ever-loving son
Frank

Jory had scrawled across the letter and forwarded it, to his solicitor:

10th March 1947

For the attention of Edward Smalley-

Frank has been a grievous disappointment to me and he can't be trusted with large amounts of money. He has had his legacy. I have checked with Edith, who has assured me she will continue with Frank's allowance as long as he needs it. Please put it on record that I do NOT intend to change my will, in case Frank (or more likely Mavis) try to challenge it after I die.

Regards,

Jory Nancarrow.

'Ok, rather brutal but to the point,' said Harriet. 'That partially answers some of our questions.'

'Let's review the list of questions we made the day before yesterday,' replied Morwenna and they both leant over the list.

1. Why did Jory Nancarrow leave his fortune to his younger daughter, Edith?
2. Why did Edith not include, Frank and Ebrel in her earlier wills? But then, as soon as Morwenna was born, Edith changed her will leaving everything to her, even though she had never met the baby?
3. Why did Edith previously leave everything to a children's home and before that, to Catherine Nicholas and who is Catherine Nicholas?
4. Why didn't Morwenna's parents and grandparents tell her anything?

'There are still a lot of gaps,' reflected Harriet.

'We know Jory didn't trust his son Frank to keep the business and house safe, so he left everything to Edith. It also looks like Jory trusted Frank's wife Mavis, even less. Edith took Catherine Nicholas from the children's home to *Gwedr Iowarth* and decided to leave the fortune to her. Then Catherine died very young in 1963. Edith changed the will again and everything was left to Helston Children's Home,' Morwenna concluded.

'We still have no idea why Edith changed the will leaving everything to you, soon after you were born or why you were never told about any of this stuff,' reflected Harriet.

'I think I have some additional information,' said Morwenna. 'Angela Smalley said the allowance payments to Frank and Mavis were stopped by Edith at the end of 1962. She suggested they may not have needed them anymore. I don't think that can be right. My grandparents lived in a rented council flat and survived off the state pension. I remember my mother and father complaining about having to lend them money at the end of each month.'

'You dad was a draftsman, wasn't he?' enquired Harriet.

'That's right. He had an adequate wage but it irritated him that he had to subsidise his parents-in-law. It was one of the few things Mum and Dad argued about because the monthly loans were never repaid,' stated Morwenna.

Ada put her head around the door and told them supper would be ready in fifteen minutes.

'Come on Titan,' Ada called to the dog. 'Come and get your dinner!'

Titan jumped up, looked apologetically at his mistress and trotted after Ada. Morwenna and Harriet used the cloakroom and made their way to the dining room.

'It's great having your meals served to you isn't it,' whispered Morwenna with a guilty smile. 'I was embarrassed at first, but I'm becoming quite used to it. The food is a bit old-fashioned but very welcome!'

'Yes, I agree,' said Harriet. 'What are you going to do when Ada leaves?'

Ada served a chicken casserole followed by sticky toffee pudding and they both tucked in. Titan slipped back into the dining room as soon as he could, and stretched out under the table with his nose resting on Morwenna's shoes. She was feeling much better and she suggested they make a start on going through things in the study the next day to look for further information. As they ate, there was a white flash of lightning and a low menacing grumble followed by a roar of thunder. The rain beat hard against the north facing windows of the dining room and Titan shivered under the table.

'Well, it looks like the weather has broken,' said Harriet, 'so we might as well spend the day indoors tomorrow.'

'I'm hoping Catherine Nicholas's foundling and death certificates will come through tomorrow as well,' said Morwenna. 'To tell you the truth, it's going to be a while before I go near that mirror again whether its sunny or not!'

'That really freaked you out, didn't it,' said Harriet. 'I went back later after you had gone and stared through the mirror for ages and nothing happened!'

'I know, I know,' Morwenna laughed. 'Just sunstroke!'

Harriet told her companion about the conversation with Joseph Penhaligon.

'Blimey, he doesn't look seventy-eight. On my first day, Ada alluded to some sort of *condition* but she didn't say it was schizophrenia. Of course, I would never throw him out of his home. You know me, Harriet. I am a soft touch!' replied Morwenna.

After supper, the two friends rested in the sitting room and watched the storm through the French windows. They were making an action plan for the next few days. Turbulent clouds filled the northern sky and little daylight remained. They had to put the lights on to allow them to see their paper-work. Harriet jumped out of her skin when there was a huge boom of thunder and forked lightening which lit the garden, like sunshine, momentarily. Morwenna shut the curtains as she felt afraid of the mirror they had uncovered and the feared seeing it, even from the house.

As the storm advanced from north to south the rain grew into a deluge. The two women transferred into the study to view the spectacle over the sea. They dragged the armchairs to the window so they could have the best view. With each flash, they could see the angry seas and the wind shook and flexed the panes of glass. Forks of lightening split the darkening sky, to be extinguished by the inky seas below. Through the tempest, Titan quivered like a coward and tried to squeeze himself between the back of Morwenna's knees and the chair.

'It's not surprising Edith slept in a bedroom overlooking the garden, these coastal rooms must be really battered by the weather in winter,' said Morwenna. 'What shall we do tomorrow if this wind and rain continues? The weather forecast isn't good.'

'We can begin reading the diaries,' suggested Harriet as she nodded towards the pile of black leather books stacked on the desk.

'It's a bit grim, but I think we need to start sorting through Edith's bedroom and personal things,' exclaimed Morwenna. 'We can't leave the house like this. It's unseemly having her things on show, all over the place.'

The two companions remained with Titan until the storm quietened. They went to bed, satisfied that they had a plan for the next day.

Chapter 7

Catherine Nicholas

Even though the storm had drifted away to the south, the rain still beat on the roof the next morning. Morwenna lay for a while in her bed, thinking about the day ahead. Bath and her difficulties with Jonathan seemed a million miles away. After walking Titan and getting absolutely drenched, she joined Harriet in the library to continue with their project. Morwenna found e-mails containing both the foundling certificate and the death certificate for Catherine Nicholas. Her friend was excited to see the documents and she anticipated a wealth of information. Before she even opened the e-mails, Morwenna cautioned Harriet that birth and death certificates did not usually contain that much detail.

First, they opened the so-called *foundling certificate* for Catherine. The approximate age was given as 'one day'. The place of birth column was crossed out in pen and replaced with 'place where found,' which read Helston Children's Home, as expected. The surname was marked 'unknown' as was the mother's maiden name. Underneath the registrar general had written that after investigation the mother could not be located and the child was given the name, 'Catherine Angela Nicholas'. The date of birth was changed to 'date found' which was 24th December 1943.

'You were right,' said Harriet with a dispirited look. 'Nothing new there.'

'You know what puzzles me Harri,' said Morwenna. 'I wonder why Catherine wasn't adopted. In the 1940's, a healthy new born baby would have been adopted, wouldn't they?'

'You worked in social services,' said Harriet. 'Maybe she had some sort of illness or disability?'

Next, Morwenna opened the attachment marked *death certificate*.

'Date of death- 1st January 1963; place of death- Gwedr Iowarth, Porthleven; age- twenty years; occupation- companion; cause of death-head trauma after a fall,' Morwenna read out loud.

'Oh, my goodness,' said Harriet. 'How horrible, on New Year's Day as well.' The two women gazed at one another. They hadn't been expecting that.

Ada had offered to help them sort through Edith's bedroom that afternoon so they decided to spend the rest of the morning in the study looking through the desk and the diaries. Before leaving the library Morwenna printed off the foundling and death certificates and added them to the stack of documents belonging to Catherine Nicholas.

It felt treacherous going through Edith's desk and Morwenna was uncomfortable with it.

'It's like snooping or prying on someone's private business,' she complained.

'But it has to be done,' Harriet reminded her companion.

Edith had been a woman with many interests and she was also untidy, so there was a lot of inconsequential things mixed with items that were important to their enquiry. In the bottom right-hand drawer, Harriet found a slim folder with the name *Catherine* on the front. She emptied the contents on to the desk.

A photograph lay on the top. On the back was the inscription, *'Catherine 1961'*. Morwenna flipped it over and they both stared at her picture. Catherine was seated at a piano, with one hand on the keyboard and the other waving at the camera. She was beautiful without a doubt.

'Well, now we know why she wasn't adopted. She was black,' said Harriet bluntly, glancing at her own skin colour.

'What an awful thing to say Harri,' said Morwenna.

'British society was very racist in the 1940's,' insisted Harriet. 'In fact, if you remember our childhood in the 1970's. People were openly racist to me. Prejudice is just a lot more subtle nowadays. Catherine looks biracial, but that would have been enough to consign her to a children's home, with little chance of adoption, back then. I encountered plenty of bigotry as a paediatrician and I've witnessed discrimination, first hand.'

'She was handsome don't you think?' continued Harriet. 'Captivating is the word I would use. Catherine has an elusive quality about her.'

'Yes, it's like she wants to draw you into the picture. What a tragic and short life she led,' said Morwenna, peering at the photograph. 'Look at the expression on her face. She has a sort of mischievous look, don't you agree?'

'Its strange how someone's personality can shine out from a photograph. I bet she was someone who loved life and make those around her joyful,' reflected Harriet sadly.

The next item was the statement from the coroner's inquest. Morwenna read it through several times and then summarised it to Harriet. The inquest in relation to Catherine had been held on 20th May 1963, in front of a jury, at the coroner's court in Truro. The coroner described that sometime in the early hours of the morning, on New Year's Day 1963, Catherine had fallen from the south terrace of *Gwedr Iowarth* and died of a head injury as she hit her head on the rocks below. The time of death was estimated to be between midnight and half past one in the morning. Her body was found on New Year's Day at around eleven in the morning by William Penhaligon, the head gardener. There was a moderate amount of alcohol in her system, but she was otherwise fit and well pre-morbidly. The ground was slippery following a snow fall which could have been a factor.

The court had considered *unlawful killing* and the police had interviewed all those attending the New Year's Eve house party at *Gwedr Iowarth*, but they found no evidence of foul-play. The coroner had also considered *suicide* because a couple of house guests had mentioned that Catherine had been unusually emotional and pre-occupied during the period between Christmas and New Year. The court could not rely on a verdict of *accidental death* because the railings protecting the south terrace from the cliff edge were sound, although a little low. Given the railings were only hip-height it was a possibility that

Catherine slipped and tumbled to her death. So, he advised the jury to return an *open verdict,* which they did.

'Look!' cried Morwenna. 'Someone has written notes on this.'

Morwenna passed the report for Harriet to examine. The extra notes were definitely in Edith's handwriting, as it matched other letters and documents they had found in her desk. Edith had drawn an arrow to the word *suicide* and written *never.* Next to the word accident she had inscribed *impossible.* At the bottom of the report Edith had scrawled the word *murder* and underlined it. Harriet frowned and pursed her lips as she read the word *murder.* She observed Morwenna, who looked horrified.

The third and final item was an article in the Cornish News Chronical. It was titled 'Double tragedy for foundling who dies in suspicious circumstances.' The article contained few facts not already known to Morwenna and Harriet. It was written in a rather salacious style referring to the tragedy of Catherine's life and a couple of openly racist comments and insinuations would never have been published nowadays. The writer described the New Year's Eve party being attended by the extended Nancarrow family and friends. Much emphasis was made on Catherine's *beguiling beauty* and possible attention from male suitors which would have been viewed as *victim-blaming* in today's terms. There was one very bland quotation from Morgan Trevethan, Morwenna's father, who was described as a family spokesman. This said; *'We would ask the press to respect our privacy at this tragic time. Catherine was Miss Edith Nancarrow's ward and companion. We all loved her like a member of our family and we wish to be left to grieve in privacy following this terrible accident.'* At the end of the article there was a request by the police for any information to help identify a trespasser observed in the grounds of *Gwedr Iowarth* on Christmas Eve. A middle-aged woman had been seen wearing an unusual short yellow quilted coat.

'Oh, my goodness,' said Harriet. 'It's a murder case. This explains the reason Gwedr Iowarth was never discussed with *you* Wenna, and why Edith stopped Frank's allowance. Your branch of the family became estranged from Edith, because they were murder suspects!'

'We must solve it Harri,' replied Morwenna passionately. 'I need to try and exonerate my family at least. Hopefully the murderer was one of the other guests?'

Just as Morwenna said, 'murderer', Ada walked into the room and announced that lunch was ready. The two women tucked into the ham salad and Ada hovered near the dining room door in a way that was unfamiliar.

'I guess you've found out about Catherine's death?' offered Ada.

'Yes,' said Morwenna looking up from her food. 'What do *you* think happened?'

'I have never been able to work it out,' replied Ada, 'but don't let it dominate your thoughts. Miss Nancarrow let it ravage her life for half a century. Many lives were ruined by Catherine's death. Believe me, it's not worth it. I don't think we will ever know what really happened.'

After Ada left the room, Harriet said, 'the words of a wise woman or someone who knows more than she says and doesn't want us looking into this further?'

As promised, the housekeeper helped Harriet and Morwenna sort through Edith's personal possessions in her bedroom that afternoon. Ada suggested starting with Edith's dressing table, tall boy and wardrobe. The housekeeper had collected empty charity bags from Helston and she suggested sorting her clothes and shoes into- *keep, charity shop and throw away.* She explained that after the infamous New Year's Eve party of 1962, Edith had led a very quiet life. She discarded most of her grander clothes or stored them on the top floor. Ada admitted that sorting out the 'top floor', as she called the servants old quarters, would be a big job. Over the last hundred years the family had a habit of storing things up there for chance they were needed. On the other hand, Edith's bedroom had scores of books and papers but not many clothes and shoes, so this wasn't going to be too difficult.

'She doesn't have much fancy foot-wear,' said Harriet who had a notable shoe fetish. 'These are mostly sensible shoes for walking and gardening.'

'No, she rarely wore high-heals or open-toe sandals because she didn't like her feet,' said Ada.

Morwenna discovered she was the same size as Edith and decided to try on a couple of pairs of new outdoor shoes. She whipped off her sandals exposing her bare feet.

'Oh, you have it too!' said Ada, pointing at Morwenna's feet.

'What?' said Morwenna self-consciously.

Harriet cringed, knowing her friend hated people to mention her 'funny feet', as she called them.

'Twin toes,' Ada said. 'Second and third toes fused. Edith had it. That's why she detested her feet.'

'Interesting,' said Harriet. 'The medical term is syndactyly. Commonly known as twin toes or webbed toes. I learned about it, in medical school.'

Ada suspected she had slightly embarrassed Morwenna so she dropped the subject of feet. The three women worked companionably for the next couple of hours. They each chose a few items to keep. Harriet selected a red silk scarf and a brooch. Ada asked for the glass dressing table set for her new house and Morwenna picked a colourful hand-knitted cardigan embellished with embroidered flowers and couple of pairs of newer outdoor shoes. They filled two bags, mainly with underwear for disposal and there were ten charity bags to carry downstairs to be dropped off in Falmouth. They stacked the paper-work and books in boxes, to be transferred to the study and included in their investigation.

Edith's bedroom was now empty except for furniture. Harriet suggested she drive the housekeeper into Falmouth on her next day off and Ada could show her where to leave the donations. Harriet thought they were going to have their work cut out over the next few weeks. In addition to sorting through over a hundred years accumulation of possessions, they were committed to a full-scale murder enquiry.

Chapter 8

The Murder Enquiry

Harriet was out of bed long before Morwenna the next morning. Her symptoms of long COVID seemed to have almost disappeared over the last few days and she was normally an early riser. Harriet had always fancied herself as an amateur sleuth and she watched many of the murder mystery programmes on television. Harriet rose at six-thirty, and she discovered Ada was also already up and finishing her breakfast at the kitchen table. She looked up in surprise as Harriet entered the room, a couple of hours before Ada had come to expect her. As usual, the housekeeper was neatly but soberly attired in a dark blue dress and flat, laced shoes. The generation gap was made more noticeable by Harriet's choice of stripy shorts and red training shoes.

'I'm usually a very earlier riser,' Harriet explained, 'but recently I've been sleeping later because of post-corona symptoms. I think the after-effects of the virus have finally gone away.'

'The Cornish air must have done you good,' Ada replied, glancing up from her breakfast.

'Ada,' asked Harriet. 'Do we have a flip chart or white board?'

'I'm not sure what you mean,' replied Ada with a puzzled expression.

'Like an easel or free-standing blackboard?'

'Ah yes. I'm with you now,' confirmed the housekeeper. 'We don't have a white board or flip chart, but I know where we have two black-boards. Will they do?'

'Yes perfect, could you show me where they are?'

Ada led her to a door at the far side of the kitchen, which Harriet had presumed was the entrance to a storage cupboard or larder.

'These are the back-stairs,' explained Ada. 'They were for the servants.'

'I didn't realise there was a second flight of stairs,' exclaimed Harriet. 'I wondered how you walked around the house and moved to and from your room without being heard or seen!'

The two women scaled the neglected spiral steps as they coiled up to the first floor. They were narrow, dingy and bare. Harriet observed the hollowing of the scuffed timber, worn away by the work shoes of weary maids clambering up and down, in the service of the Nancarrow family. The back-stairs were a far cry from the wide mahogany staircase that graced the main house. At the top of the initial flight, Ada pointed to a door and she explained that it emerged into the linen cupboard on the first-floor landing. Harriet and her older companion clattered up the second flight to reach the top floor of the house which contained the servants' quarters.

'Where are we heading for?' puffed Harriet, who was now out of breath.

'The nursery,' explained Ada. 'It hasn't been occupied for years. Miss Nancarrow was the last child to use the nursery and take lessons in the schoolroom, long before my time. I'm afraid there are also quite a lot of things stored up here.'

'I'm sorry to tell you that there is even more clutter in the attic,' said the older woman nodding towards the roof. 'I think that's where the really ancient stuff is.'

'How many staff were there when you came here?' asked Harriet. She didn't like to us the word *servants*.

'Just me living in the house. By the 1960s the cook and the house-keeper lived in the village and came to the house daily. William Penhaligon was the head gardener and he lived in the cottage with Joseph,' recalled Ada.

The nursery was located at the north side of the house, above the master bedroom which Edith had previously occupied. It consisted of a small suite of rooms including a central play room. Off the playroom was one small bedroom, one large bedroom and a schoolroom. Ada explained that the smaller bedroom was for *Nanny*, and the larger bedroom was for the children. The playroom doubled as a sitting room for the nanny once her charges were in bed. Ada showed Harriet the bars on the windows.

'You can always spot the nursery in an old house because of the bars on the windows, to stop the children falling out,' explained Ada, who had read many of the social history books in the Nancarrow library.

Although there were several boxes stored near the entrance to the nursery, the rest of the room was clear and also quite eerie, Harriet thought. The nursery looked like it had been largely left undisturbed since Edith had been a child in the 1920s. There were toys on the floor of the playroom and desks, books and a globe in the schoolroom and so on. Harriet ran her fingers through the dust on the top of the extravagant doll's house as she followed the housekeeper. They headed directly to the schoolroom and Ada nodded towards two free standing blackboards on hinged A-frames.

'Will these do?' she asked.

'Absolutely perfect,' replied Harriet.

'The chalk's probably a hundred years old, but I'm sure it still works,' laughed Ada.

Harriet assured Ada that she could manage from now. She didn't want the older woman carrying heavy blackboards downstairs and she didn't need too many probing questions at this stage. After all, Ada herself could well be a suspect in the murder enquiry. So, the house-keeper retraced her steps down the back-stairs and Harriet was left in the nursery alone. She put a box of multi-coloured chalks in her pocket for later. She wondered if Morwenna knew about the back-stairs and suspected that she probably didn't.

Harriet lifted the smaller blackboard and heaved it down the main staircase to the first floor. She leant it against the wall and paused for a minute to get her breath back. Harriet re-traced her steps and retrieved the larger blackboard, and left it next to the first. She had a quick peak in the linen cupboard on the landing and saw the concealed door to the back-stairs. So that's how the servants accessed the main bedrooms to clean them and light fires without disturbing the family downstairs in days gone by, ingenious, she thought. How she envied wealthy people in the 1800s although she suspected she wouldn't have coped very well with gender roles of women in those days.

Harriet lugged the blackboards down the second staircase, one at a time, and into the library, which was going to be the centre of operations. She erected them at the head of the large table so that she and Morwenna would be able to see their findings readily. On the smaller board she wrote *motive, means and opportunity* and on the second board she wrote *suspects*.

Harriet glanced at her watch which read eight o'clock and simultaneously she heard Titan woof a few barks of welcome, as Morwenna came down the stairs into the hall. There was an inviting smell of bacon and eggs emerging from the dining room, so the two women guessed breakfast was ready. Ada had already set the portions of cooked breakfast, tea and toast on the table, so they tucked in. Shortly the housekeeper entered, to retrieve the plates.

'Could one of you drop me off in Falmouth this morning?' Ada asked. 'The charity shops have re-opened after lockdown and they are taking donations, so we can drop off the bags. Also, the tenants have left my house and I want to have a look at the property to see what needs doing before I move in. I can take the bus back.'

Harriet experienced a spark of impatience at not being able to start on their investigation straight away, so she suggested that she could drop Ada off in Falmouth, while Morwenna took Titan for a walk. That way they would save time, as it would be an hour's round trip to transport Ada and the bags to Falmouth.

It was just after eleven when the two companions entered the library to start work. Morwenna was very impressed with the blackboards. Before they began, Harriet told her friend about the back-staircase. Harriet had been correct; her friend had not been aware of its existence. She was immediately curious and so Harriet led her the stairwell in the kitchen storeroom. Harriet also revealed the concealed entrance to the back-stairs from the linen cupboard on the landing of the first floor.

They conducted a brief inspection of the top floor including the nursery and took a glance in Ada's bedroom. The room was rather spartan but very clean and orderly. There was a neat tower of books stacked by empty tea-chests, presumably Ada was preparing for her move to Falmouth.

'*Mansfield Park, Agnes Grey and Chromosomal and DNA Analysis in Human Genealogy*,' read Harriet out loud, as she examined the books nearest her reach.

'A sophisticated choice of literature for a housekeeper,' remarked Morwenna.

'I wouldn't know. I've never heard of the first two titles,' admitted Harriet.

'Honestly Harri, don't you read? enquired Morwenna.

'I've read all Annie S Azzor's books. *Trouble* is my favourite,' replied Harriet.

'Now you've retired you could try a bit of period literature such as Austen or the Brontës?' suggested her friend.

'Good idea. Once we've solved this murder,' said Harriet. 'I have a stack of books by Victoria C Hamish at home. I like a good bodice-ripper!'

Morwenna, being a diplomat and a kindly person, politely chose *not* to comment further on Harriet's literary interests. The two women viewed the nursery and they peered into the other bedrooms on the top floor. Other than the nursery and Ada's room, the bedrooms were crammed with boxes and trunks. Harriet told her companion what the housekeeper had said about the *really old stuff in the attic*.

'Blimey,' said Morwenna. 'It may become my life's work to sort through all these possessions.'

'No wonder Ada was keen for us to drop the first consignment off at the charity shop,' replied Harriet. 'This could take years.'

Together, they returned to the library and started to populate the two blackboards.

'*How? Why? Who?*' said Harriet in a staccato voice, while tapping the smaller blackboard with her pen.

Harriet wrote: Catherine aged twenty, died between midnight and one-thirty on 1st January 1963. Cause of death was falling from the south terrace and hitting her head on the rocks below.

'Possible motives for murder are as follows,' continued Harriet, pointing at the second blackboard.

'What do you mean?' asked her friend.

'Lust, love, anger, hatred, envy, money and madness,' said Harriet, in full sleuthing stride now.

'And the *who*?' enquired Morwenna.

'For that, we need to find out who lived here and who was at the New Year's Eve party,' concluded Harriet.

Harriet started to make a list on the larger blackboard under the heading 'suspects':

She wrote down Edith Nancarrow and Ada Bray first of all.

'We know your father was here because he gave a statement to the press,' said Harriet, so she added the name Morgan Trevethan.

'And I'm guessing your mother,' and she wrote Ebrel Trevethan on the blackboard.

Harriet then added Frank and Mavis Nancarrow as the wider family was referred to in the coroner's report. She also recorded William Penhaligon and Joseph Panhaligon and friends- *to be determined*.

'Ada said there was a housekeeper and a cook but they lived in the village,' recalled Harriet. 'I'm guessing they would have gone home but we need to check that.'

'Don't forget to add the woman trespasser. The one who was spotted on Christmas Eve, she might have come back to kill Catherine,' said Morwenna.

Harriet scrawled, *middle aged woman with short quilted coat*, on the tally of suspects.

'Well, that's a start,' said Morwenna, resting her chin on her fists and peering with determination at the list of names. 'Let's have lunch and then see if Edith's diaries can help us?'

Chapter 9

The Letter

After lunch, Harriet and Morwenna returned to the study to retrieve the diaries from the safe. They carried the weighty volumes to the library and stacked them, in date order, on the table. There was an edition for each year from 1935 to 1963, although the War years were missing.

'We probably need to read all of these, but let's start with December 1962,' said Morwenna. 'That's the month leading up to Catherine's death.'

She lifted the 1962 diary and proceeded directly to the page for 31st December, which was blank. Between the empty page and the leather outer cover, nestled a sealed letter addressed to Morwenna Trevethan.

'Oh, my goodness,' said Harriet. 'How weird is that?'

Harriet held her breath in excitement, as her companion gingerly eased open the envelope with her thumb. She extracted three large sheets of fragile cream writing paper. She read the letter aloud.

24th June 1987

Dear Morwenna,

I write to you on the occasion of your twenty-first birthday. You won't see this letter until I die, which hopefully won't be for a good few years yet! I made a conscious decision to stay out of your life because of the terrible rift between the two branches of our family and my fear of making an already tragic situation worse.

I have kept tabs on you for the last twenty-one years by using a private investigator. Sorry! I'll leave you alone from now onwards, I promise. I just wanted to make sure you had become the sort of person who could cope with inheriting Gwedr Iowarth, and all that goes with it.

At the time I write this letter you have just qualified as a social worker and you are working in your chosen field of fostering and adoption, a cause very close to my heart. As you go through my things, you will gather I was closely involved with supporting Helston Children's Home and I took a special interest in some of the children who resided there.

The fact that you have opened the page of my diary for 31st January 1962 means you know about Catherine's death and you want to find out what really happened. Maybe, with modern methods such as computers or DNA, you can find out who killed my lovely ward, Catherine, please try. I can assure you she would never have committed suicide and I don't believe her death was an accident.

You are probably thinking the motive for her murder was financial, perhaps a member of our family wanted Catherine out of the way so she could not inherit the house and the money. However, it's important that you understand that neither Catherine, nor any member of the family, was informed that I had left Gwedr Iowarth and the estate to her. Only my solicitor knew about the will bequeathing everything to Catherine and he is one hundred percent trustworthy. The sole copy of the will was kept in the solicitor's office and not at the house. I didn't want to cause further bad feeling in the family and I wanted to protect Catherine, so I always insinuated that all the wider family would benefit when I died, so there could have been no financial motive to harm Catherine.

As you will gather from the press and the police reports, there were rumours about Catherine's relationships with men but she was a typical inexperienced nineteen-year-old, although

65

stunningly beautiful. I can't see Jonathan, Emily or Phillipe ever harming her even though she did kiss Jonathan on Christmas Eve, which caused a lot of trouble with the Watson family at the time. The police conducted a thorough enquiry and they even investigated Joseph Penhaligon because of his mental illness but I don't think he would ever have harmed Catherine. They had been childhood friends, since Catherine came to live with me when she was thirteen. The police never found the identity of the woman trespasser William Penhaligon chased out of the grounds on Christmas Eve. I can't help thinking she might have been significant. Maybe she knew Catherine and returned on New Year's Eve to kill her, having been thwarted on Christmas Eve?

After Catherine was killed, I couldn't be sure who had a hand in her death so I left my estate to Helston Children's Home to ensure the killer or killers could not benefit from her murder. However, in my heart, I wanted my home and the estate, to stay in the family and, unlike the rest of my family and friends, I was sure you could have played no part in Catherine's death. That's why I changed my will when you were born. Make sure you enjoy Gwedr Iowarth as much as I intend to do, now I have handed the house and its mysteries over to you to solve. I have every faith in you Morwenna, to catch the killer so Catherine can rest in peace. Her grave is in Porthleven Cemetery. Please visit from time to time.

With love,
Edith Nancarrow

Morwenna and Harriet leant forward in their seats and regarded each other, aghast.

'This is so eerie,' said Harriet. 'It's like Edith knew you would come here and solve this mystery for her.'

'Harri, she had me trailed by private investigator until I was twenty-one,' breathed Morwenna. 'She must have gathered information about my personality as well as what I was doing.'

'It seems that Edith transferred this investigation over to you in 1987, when you were twenty-one, and that allowed her some peace to proceed with the rest of her life,' thought Harriet out loud.

'Well, I'm not going to let her down. Let's get on with it,' announced Morwenna with iron intensity as she banged her fist on the table.

Harriet turned to her suspects on the blackboard and added the names, *Jonathan, Emily and Phillipe.*

'We are probably going to have to ask Ada about some of this soon,' said Harriet.

'Yes, I agree,' replied her companion. 'But she's not here, so let's go through the diaries and see what we can find out.'

Morwenna left to prepare coffee, while Harriet began reading the entries from December 1962, to see if she could find anything more about the new suspects. It became clear to Harriet that Edith was a little haphazard about writing her diary. Sometimes several pages were empty and other times she wrote a full page and added extra paper with tape. The entry for 27th December 1962 proved helpful. Edith had made an account of her intention to invite Phillipe Bouvier to her New Year party. She described him as the *new Canadian school teacher,* who was working at Porthleven Council School. Edith had stated her hope that he would provide a, 'suitable diversion for Catherine.' Harriet rose from her seat and added Phillipe Bouvier, school teacher, to her list of suspects.

'Probably French-Canadian,' said Morwenna who had returned to the room with their drinks.

Harriet persisted with the diaries and Morwenna searched for Phillipe Bouvier and Porthleven Council School using the internet. There was nothing about a Phillipe Bouvier on the school website. The school was now re-named *Porthleven Community Primary School.* Previous head-teachers and long-standing staff were described in the historical section but Mr Bouvier was not mentioned. Morwenna suspected the name Phillipe Bouvier would not be that common in Canada so she turned to her genealogy website. Edith had suggested he could have been of romantic interest to Catherine, so she guessed he would have been between twenty-one and thirty-one. After all, he was a qualified teacher so Phillipe must have finished college.

'Got him,' cried Morwenna, 'Phillipe Louis Bouvier, school teacher, born 2nd November 1934 in Montreal, Canada.'

'How can you be sure its him?' enquired Harriet, looking up from the diaries.

'There are only three Phillipe Bouviers born in Canada, one was born in 1903 who would be far too old and the other in 1965 so that rules him out. There were quite a few born in France, of course, but we know this guy is Canadian.'

'Clever,' replied Harriet, 'I like that family history website you use. I think I might start investigating my ancestors. I could be descended from royalty, for all I know.'

'What *do* you know about your past Harri?' asked Morwenna.

'Not much really. My mother's family have lived in Yorkshire for generations. My father came to the UK from Jamaica in the late 1950s. He ended up in Leeds working in construction, which is where he met my mother,' said Harriet.

'What about your Jamaican family? I remember you once visited when we were in the sixth form,' recalled Morwenna. 'We were all really jealous.'

'My father saved up for that trip for a couple of years. He wanted my mother and I to see his home and meet some of his relatives. It's a distant memory now. My grandparents died not long after that holiday. I receive Christmas cards from some of my cousins and that's about it,' explained Harriet.

'How did your ancestors arrive in Jamaica. Were they slaves?' asked Morwenna.

'Yes, my father told me he was descended from a slave family who worked on a sugar plantation near Montego Bay,' replied Harriet. 'But as for their African origins, I don't know. Where would you start with that?'

'Did he tell you anything else?' enquired Morwenna.

'Actually, he did say one thing, that sticks in my mind. Our surname is *Duncan* because that was the Christian name of the plantation owner,' said Harriet.

'I guess people had to relinquish their own identity when they became a slave,' said Morwenna. 'I think most slaves were abducted in West Africa. I read in my genealogy magazine that DNA analysis can be very useful in locating the region of African ancestors. A guy in the magazine had traced his ancestry right back to a woman who was abducted in Nigeria and transported to Jamaica in about 1800.'

'When we've solved your family mystery, perhaps we can start on mine?' suggested Harriet.

The women returned to the task in hand and added Phillipe Louis Bouvier, school teacher aged twenty-eight, to the information on the black board. Morwenna continued with the diaries and she found an entry on 30th December 1962. Edith had recorded that she had to telephone Dr Fred Watson to come over and stitch Catherine's foot. Apparently, her ward had been out walking with Frank Nancarrow. She had slipped on the rocks, while on the beach below the south terrace. A shard of rock had pierced her ankle causing a nasty cut. Frank had to remove her socks and shoes and bandage her foot in his scarf to stop the bleeding. He ran to fetch William Penhaligon and they had carried Catherine back to the house. Dr Watson had been called to tend to the wound. Edith recorded that the doctor had promised to re-examine the wound the following day when he attended the New Year's Eve party but sadly Catherine wouldn't be doing any dancing.

'Ok Harri,' said Morwenna. 'You can add Dr Fred Watson to the list of suspects. He was at the New Year's Eve party.'

Morwenna and Harriet agreed that they would ask Ada to clarify if anyone else was at *Gwedr Iowarth* that night.

Chapter 10

A Shock for Morwenna

After dinner, Ada entered the dining room to collect the plates. Morwenna asked her if she would join them in the library to assist with the naming of suspects. The housekeeper looked reticent but resigned. She re-iterated that she thought delving back into the past would be fruitless and potentially distressing for Morwenna. Ada reluctantly followed the two companions and Titan across the hall into the library. She had already discretely observed the blackboards while Harriet and Morwenna had been preparing for dinner, so she knew what was coming.

Harriet nodded to Ada and she perched on the edge one of the library chairs.

'Are you really sure you want to do this?' implored Ada, looking exceedingly serious.

'I am certain,' replied Morwenna. 'I need to get to the bottom of this.'

Ada recalled that the cook and housekeeper had left Gwedr Iowarth at around nine o'clock in the evening, on New Year's Eve in 1962, so they were not present when Catherine died. She confirmed that all the Nancarrow family were visiting the house over the Christmas and New Year period. This included Edith Nancarrow, Frank and Mavis Nancarrow (Morwenna's grandparents) and Morgan and Ebrel Trevethan (Morwenna's parents). Morgan and Ebrel were newly-weds, having only married six months earlier. The housekeeper declared that she was in the house on the night in question, although she had retired to bed at about ten in the evening. Ada had been a servant, only fifteen years old and not included in the festivities. She had gone to her bedroom after she had assisted the cook to tidy up after dinner and they had laid out drinks in the hall. The party was expected to continue into the early hours of the next morning.

Ada remembered that the police had also expressed an interest in the head gardener William Penhaligon and his son Joseph who, whilst not at the party, were in Gwedr Iowarth Cottage very close by. Ada recalled that the other guests included Dr Frederick Watson, the family GP and his daughter Emily Watson. She also recollected Phillipe Bouvier being present and Emily's fiancée, Jonathan.

'Ah yes, we have found Phillipe Bouvier on the genealogy site, he was a Canadian school teacher,' clarified Morwenna.

What about Jonathan?' asked Morwenna.

'Oh, he was a lodger here,' replied Ada. 'He was trainee manager at *Margins Bank* in Truro.'

'Edith was pretty well off, why did she have a lodger?' asked Harriet bluntly.

'Oh, Miss Nancarrow didn't need the money. Jonathan's parents were friends of Miss Nancarrow. So, when he started the trainee bank manager position in Truro, they asked if he could stay here. It was too far for him to travel to work in Truro from his home in Somerset each day,' explained Ada who was now rising from edge of her seat. Her body posture indicated she wanted to leave the room as soon as possible.

'I'd better get back to the dishes,' said Ada, who was trying to escape and avoid further interrogation.

'Sorry, just one more question. Jonathan's surname?' asked Harriet, holding the chalk expectantly.

The housekeeper swallowed hard and bit her lip. After what seemed like hours, Ada murmured, 'Coutts.' Her utterance was whispered and difficult to hear clearly.

Harriet stopped writing, leaving the tip of the chalk motionless, and said, 'Are you telling me he was called Jonathan *Coutts*?'

The housekeeper nodded her head slowly and Harriet recalled Ada's face when she had called Morwenna, Mrs Coutts, a couple of days earlier, after the phone call from the solicitor. Harriet knew that this was when Ada had realised the gravity of her friend's current situation. Harriet had assumed that the housekeeper was offended by Harriet calling Morwenna the, *lady of the house*. In fact, it was at this moment that Ada had realised that Morwenna was now married to Jonathan Coutts, probably the same Jonathan Coutts who had been Edith's lodger in 1962 and Emily Watson's fiancé.

'Ada, surely you are not suggesting that my husband was present in this house in 1962?' demanded Morwenna.

'I can't be certain,' said Ada, 'but it looks like it.'

Harriet thanked Ada for her honesty and suggested she leave Morwenna and her alone. The housekeeper hurried out of the room, without even a backwards glance. Morwenna pressed her fists into the seat of the chair and clenched her teeth. Harriet turned to the computer, while her companion brooded in silence. It took a minimal amount of research on the internet for Harriet to confirm that Margins Bank had merged with Bradders in 1989. There was a strong possibility that Morwenna's husband had, indeed, been present at Gwedr Iowarth at the time of Catherine's death.

The two women sat quietly, in their respective seats around the library table, for a few moments. Morwenna's chin drooped and she rested her forehead on her heal of her hands. Harriet knew she should not interrupt, and so she poured them both a double brandy. The two women gulped the liquor while Morwenna tried to quell a chaos of emotions. Harriet privately considered what to do next. She elected to allow her companion to start the conversation, when she had the presence of mind to speak. Presently they talked and turned over the possibilities.

'Oh, my goodness Harri,' said Morwenna, who was deathly pale. 'This throws my whole marriage up in the air.'

'This is my fault,' cried Harriet. 'I should never have pushed this inquiry.'

'No wonder Jonathan didn't want me to look into my past. He didn't want me to come here! My husband could be a murderer. Maybe he came looking for me ten years ago and married me because he knew I would inherit this estate,' said Morwenna, sweeping her arm around the room.

'This is worse than awful,' shouted Harriet passionate now, forgetting her private undertaking to keep calm and reasonable. 'We need to phone Jonathan and ask him what the hell is going on!'

'We can't,' replied Morwenna. 'He's in the outback with his son-in-law and there's no mobile phone connection. This could be some sort of weird coincidence and *my* Jonathan might have nothing to do with it.'

'If it is *your* Jonathan, we could just walk away,' said Harriet. 'You could sell the house and take the inheritance. That way, he need never be aware of what we found out.'

'Harri, I have to know. I owe it to Edith and Catherine and I owe it to myself,' replied Morwenna, raising her chin in the air obstinately. 'If we verify that *my* Jonathan was here in 1962, we will still press on with the investigation.'

'Look, Wenna,' said Harriet softly. She was calmer now. 'I've known Jonathan for a few years. He's about the best-humoured man, a person could meet. He's a decent guy and certainly not a murderer. I know this looks really serious, but let's go to bed, get some sleep and then check things out in the morning.'

'You're right. We can't do anything now,' replied Morwenna.

Titan put his head on his mistress's lap and then reached up to licked her face.

'Things might seem better in the morning,' said Morwenna bravely, although the strain on her face told a different story.

'That's the spirit,' encouraged Harriet, and they both climbed the stairs to bed.

Chapter 11

Jonathan

Morwenna finally fell into a broken slumber in the early hours of the morning. In spite of finding some shallow spells of sleep, her dreams were feverish and crowded with tormented images. She awoke numerous times, wondering about Jonathan's part in this tragedy, and whether he sensed her terrible discovery and perceived her pain.

Harriet also spent a fretful night. She turned fitfully, trying to work out what to do for the best. Her main concern was her friend's, already fragile, state of mind. Harriet awoke with the twittering of birds, the sheets tangled around her legs and the duvet on the floor. She formulated a plan in her mind to obtain the information they needed to establish whether Morwenna's husband had been at Gwedr Iowarth in 1962. She took her lap-top down to Ada who was working in the kitchen.

'Morning Ada,' said Harriet.

'Morning,' replied the older woman grimly.

Ada made Harriet a cup of coffee, in silence, and placed it on the table.

'This isn't your fault,' said Harriet. 'We insisted you told us and you couldn't lie. We would have found out in the end anyway.'

'That's true, but I feel terrible. The solicitor told me that Morwenna was called Trevethan. I only heard the surname Coutts the other day, in the dining room, when you called her Mrs Coutts. I wondered about telling you there and then but I decided against it. I spent several hours in utter torment after I realised what I had discovered. I hoped you two would become bored with the investigation and it might never come out. I even prayed it wasn't the same Jonathan Coutts.'

'Look, here's a photo of Jonathan on his wedding day with Morwenna,' said Harriet pointing to the screen on her lap top. 'Does it look like him?'

'I'm almost sure it's him,' said Ada, looking at the picture and nodding her head.

Just after nine in the morning, Harriet rang the investment office of Bradders Bank in London where Jonathan used to work. She was a very good mimic and she had the same Yorkshire accent as her friend anyway. Harriet pretended to be Morwenna and she was put through to Jonathan's former colleague, Frederick Forster, who Harriet had previously met at a dinner party.

'Hi Fred,' said Harriet. 'Morwenna Coutts here, Jonathan's wife.'

'Wow Morwenna, nice to hear from you. It's been ages, are you both OK?'

'You know poor Jonathan has been stranded in Australia,' said Harriet after a little small-talk. 'Well, he's managed to book a flight back to the UK and I'm planning a remote theme-party, like an online celebration of his life. Could you have a look in the personnel records and check whether he was assistant manager at Margins bank in Truro, before Margins merged with Bradders? I have a feeling he once mentioned that he was in Truro. Back in the sixties.'

'No problem,' said Fred. 'I can probably send you a few anecdotes as well.'

'Brilliant,' said Harriet and she told Fred her e-mail address.

'Hope I receive an invite to the online event,' replied Fred. 'I've not heard of this type of party before. It sounds like fun.'

'Yes definitely, Fred,' lied Harriet and put the phone down.

Morwenna arose from her bed at around ten in the morning and soon after that Harriet received the e-mail from Fred Forster which confirmed their worst fears. Morwenna was indeed married to the same Jonathan Coutts who had been a lodger at Gwedr Iowarth and Emily Watson's fiancée in 1962. Harriet had also established from Ada that Emily Watson was still alive and residing in Helston so they had another witness.

'Are you sure you want to carry on with this?' asked Harriet of her weary-looking friend.

'I have to Harriet,' said Morwenna with an anguished expression. 'I've been up half the night thinking about it. Jonathan is the best thing that ever happened to me. The last ten years have been the happiest of my life. I won't be able to live a lie, so I'm going to have to get to the truth.'

Morwenna forced down a piece of toast and a cup of coffee at Harriet's insistence and searched for a ploy to distract her.

'Ok Wenna,' said Harriet. 'Let's take Titan out for a walk, clear our heads and make a plan.'

'We can have a stroll around the garden first,' suggested Morwenna.

The two sombre companions proceeded to the kitchen. The scene visualised through the window revealed an azure sky. Morwenna dropped Titan's leash in her pocket, as it wouldn't be needed until they were on the road. She knew the dog well now, and he never ran away from her. She was not a person to accept defeat, so she set forth through the balmy air, with a feigned spring in her step. Her subterfuge was impressive, considering how wretched she felt inside. Morwenna was efficient at concealing her feelings. After all she had spent half a century in this endeavour.

After leaving the kitchen and turning left, they completed a circuit of the gardens. They passed the shed and summer house and both glanced in the direction of the mirror they had cleared. Morwenna would not look directly at the mirror after what had happened last time even though Harriet encouraged her to.

'Honestly Wenna,' said Harriet, 'I stared right into it for ages and I saw and felt nothing.'

'I understand you are not a very spiritual person Harri,' replied Morwenna. 'Don't call me crazy, but I think the mirrors are like a window to the past. Perhaps I can see something of 1962 or 1963?'

They stopped next to the mirror, although Morwenna insisted on keeping her back to it.

'You told me you saw a girl with black hair, wearing a white hooded cloak,' said Harriet.

'Don't you see, that could have been Catherine?' replied Morwenna.

'Did they wear cloaks in the 1960s?' asked Harriet. 'Look I don't think we can solve this through the spirit world Wenna. It's interviews with witnesses, diaries, papers and facts that will sort this out.'

'Maybe,' said Morwenna, 'but we may have to try anything now the stakes are so high.'

The women and Titan set off again, passing the west side of the house and emerging on the south terrace. Morwenna walked up to the railings and stared down the cliff to the rocks below. Harriet was scared of heights and held back.

'I don't see how anyone could fall over these railings accidently,' concluded Morwenna, 'even if they were drunk. Look they are chest height and very sturdy.'

'Miss Nancarrow had those railings replaced after Catherine died,' came the voice of Joseph Penhaligon as he emerged from around the side of the house.'

'Oh blimey!' said Harriet spinning around to face Joseph, 'Where did you come from? You startled me.'

'Sorry. The old railings were very strong too, but only waist height,' continued Joseph. 'Ada told me you are looking into Catherine's death again. I'll help you if I can.'

'Thanks, so much Joseph,' interjected Morwenna. 'We *are* going to need help.'

'I never thought it was an accident,' said Joseph, with intensity. 'I knew Catherine when she came here. I was fourteen and she was thirteen, when she first arrived from the children's home.'

'Could we come over and talk to you about it?' asked Harriet forthrightly.

'Yes, of course. It was a terrible time for me 1962. Probably do me good to talk about it. My doctor keeps offering me *psychotherapy*, as he calls it. Tell you what, come over to the cottage tomorrow afternoon.'

The two companions agreed to Joseph's suggestion and they made their way towards Porthleven. Titan trotted forward and Morwenna attached his lead. As they climbed down the hill, they formulated plan of action. Harriet suggested they interview each living witness so this would include Ada Bray, Joseph Penhaligon, Emily Watson and Jonathan. Ironically Jonathan was the only one they did not have access to currently, so they would have to concentrate on the other three. They also needed to update their suspect board with the new information that had come to light over the last twenty-four hours. They covered a circuit of the town and felt much more positive by the time they returned to the house.

Ada brought lunch to the dining room at one o'clock and she readily agreed to be interviewed about Catherine's death. She also produced a slip of paper with Emily Watson's address and phone number on it.

'Ada is acting pretty relaxed now,' said Harriet, after the housekeeper had cleared the table and left the room.

'I think she was holding back because she had guessed Jonathan's identity. However, she is *still* a suspect,' replied Morwenna firmly.

The two companions returned to the library and updated the suspect board with recent facts they had acquired. They decided that Harriet would contact Emily Watson and request a meeting. Harriet thought it would be a bit uncomfortable for Morwenna to speak to Emily as Emily was Jonathan's ex-fiancée. Also, Emily may not talk openly to Morwenna, given her current connection with Jonathan. Morwenna decided to undertake the meeting with Joseph Penhaligon the following afternoon.

They debated how best to approach Emily Watson, as she could easily refuse to speak to them, especially if she was guilty of any wrong-doing. Harriet phoned her and introduced herself as Harriet Duncan and she explained that she was helping a friend sort out Edith Nancarrow's affairs after her death and asked if she could visit to gather some information. Emily sounded curious, not defensive, on the phone and agreed to Harriet calling on her the next afternoon.

Harriet and Morwenna spent the rest of the day conducting research on Emily. The genealogy website informed them that she had never married and had no children. A local newspaper article, following her retirement in 2002, recorded that she had attended Bingley Teacher Training College in Yorkshire in 1965 and trained to be a history teacher. Emily had then worked at a school in Kenya for two years, as a junior mistress. She returned to Cornwall in 1970 and took up a post in an all-girls boarding school, in Truro, where she was emplyed as a house mistress and then deputy head until her retirement. There were a couple of tributes to her on the school website, describing her as a *dedicated teacher* and *her girls being her life.*

'She doesn't sound like a murderer,' said Morwenna.

'You can't be sure,' reflected Harriet. 'Look at some of the teachers we had. They looked pretty respectable on the outside but they could be quite evil. Remember Miss Fuller, the PE teacher. A psychopath that one!'

'Yes, I see what you mean,' said Morwenna laughing for the first time that day.

After dinner, Morwenna and Harriet were emotionally exhausted. They decided to leave the investigation alone for a few hours and had a game of Scrabble before bed. Usually, Morwenna could beat Harriet easily, but she was pre-occupied and overtired that evening. Harriet won the game by over a hundred points and she put her success down to her friend's shock discovery about Jonathan and lack of sleep. By half past nine they both retired to bed.

Chapter 12

Morwenna Takes Things into Her Own Hands

Now that the stakes were so high Morwenna was emboldened. She had secretly decided to re-visit the mirror to explore what she could learn about Catherine's death. The only question was, when she would have the courage to do it.

After the game of Scrabble, Morwenna perched on the edge of her bed and pondered recent events before approaching the window. Her bedroom was situated over the morning room and faced due south. She crouched inquisitively by the window and watched. After a while her vision to adjusted to the failing light. It was twilight but she could still see the south terrace below and the outdoor furniture. Beyond that, she could make out the railings guarding the cliff. She imagined that someone could have seen, or possibly heard something when Catherine fell to her death, even though it would have been dark. It would be important to establish who was occupying each room on New Year's Eve of 1962 and what time they went to bed.

By half past ten it was completely dark, but it was possible for Morwenna to see the outline of the terrace and the shape of the furniture because the drive into Gwedr Iowarth was lit by lamps on either side of the gate posts. These cast some minimal illumination over the south terrace. She wondered if the lights were there in 1962? Morwenna tugged open the sash-window and listened. Her mood was calmed by the gentle murmur of the waves.

'Ok be brave,' she whispered to herself. 'You're not going to sleep anyway tonight, so you might as well do it.'

Morwenna was well known for possessing a cautious nature, but on this occasion, desperation made her reckless. The house was quiet and she knew everyone was in bed, so she crept out of her room and tiptoed down the main staircase collecting Titan en route. He was lying in his usual spot on the rug in the stairwell and he yelped his appreciation of her visit. Morwenna shushed him and he appeared to understand that she needed to keep quiet. He trotted by her side and they entered the kitchen. She pulled on her walking shoes and yellow puffer jacket. Harriet always teased her about the coat, stating it was a hideous colour, like nicotine. There were several torches on the shelf by the back door and Morwenna took one and checked that it worked. She helped herself to the key, which had been left on its usual hook, and opened the door.

Morwenna turned left out of the back door and continued until she passed the shed and summer house. The dog clung close to her side and she rested her left hand on his bony shoulder. He seemed rather pleased to have an unexpected evening walk. Her heart thumped rapidly in her chest and she was full of nerves. She kept reminding herself that she needed to do this, to prove Jonathan's innocence. The problem was that she didn't know exactly where things were taking her, or what she needed to do.

She headed straight for the mirror that she and Harriet had exposed earlier that week. She braced herself, hoping that she would not faint again. She bit her lip and tugged her fingers, hoping that the adrenaline would help maintain her courage. Initially Morwenna kept her back to the mirror and put her hand on Titan's head, instructing him to sit and stay. She glanced at her watch with the torch. It was quarter to eleven.

Morwenna turned to face the mirror with the flashlight pointing downwards. Gradually, she raised the torch. An icy wind rushed from the mirror and she had a strong impulse to move forwards, like she was being drawn by a magnet. She held the torch in her right hand and advanced her left-hand expecting to touch the glass, but she detected nothing. She urged herself to keep moving, even though she felt light-headed. Morwenna progressed through the mirror with no resistance and found herself in the snow-covered garden of Gwedr Iowrth. Looking behind her, she could see Titan sitting obediently on the other side. She crept forwards and then crouched for a few minutes behind a garden bench, to find her bearings.

Although it was now winter and it was snowy underfoot, the house and garden were familiar and easily recognisable. Morwenna wasn't sure if she could *be* seen so she tried to keep to the shadows. Her legs were shaky but they conveyed her, intuitively, in spite of the darkness. As she approached the French-doors of the sitting room, she could hear singing voices and see bright lights inside and she stole closer to the window. The curtains were almost fully drawn but there was a gap of about six inches allowing her to observe the interior of the room. The Christmas tree was decorated with coloured lights and a group of young people were gathered around the piano singing carols. She checked her watch against the grandfather clock and the time was the same, five to eleven. She was too far away to see any other details on the clock.

It was easy to identify Catherine Nicholas, a stunning black girl playing the piano with her plentiful black hair piled up in a fashionable beehive. She was wearing a bright red, woollen fitted dress and all eyes were on her. Standing behind her and facing toward the French window was a very young-looking Jonathan. A short and rather stout young woman with curly mid-brown hair had her back to the window. She was wearing a tweed suit, old fashioned even by the standards of 1962. Probably Emily Watson, thought Morwenna. The remaining young man, looked a little older than the others and was dressed in a rather suave dark suit with a thin tie and she guessed he was Phillipe Bouvier.

After a while, they stopped singing and Phillipe went over to a record player. The strains of *Love me do,* drifted outside and they all started to dance. While the music was playing loudly, Morwenna gently tried the door handle and found it was unlocked. She opened it slightly so she could hear better. She loved dancing and experienced an unexpected urge to join their frivolities, but of course she didn't. The song finished and Phillipe and Emily complained that they were thirsty and left the room to find more drinks. Morwenna kept still and calm and strained to listen to the conversation.

While Phillipe and Emily were away, Jonathan moved closer to Catherine, caressed her shoulder and whispered, 'happy birthday.'

He kissed her briefly on the lips and murmured, 'look Catherine, I do think you are lovely but our little fling is going to have to stop.'

'But I really like you Jonathan,' she replied.

'Phillipe has the hots for you as well, so he could be your guy.'

'I'm not interested in Phillipe, as you well know,' barked Catherine.

'Well, it has to end. I'll be in serious bother with Emily if she catches wind of any of this,' pleaded Jonathan with a suggestion of anxiety in his voice.

'I could tell her if I wanted,' replied Catherine petulantly.

'You wouldn't, not on Christmas Eve …'

As Morwenna processed the horrifying implications of what she was hearing, an ice-cold dread engulfed her senses. Her vision became foggy and the contents of the room obscured.

She caught nothing further of the conversation because suddenly, she heard a man shouting behind her. Morwenna turned around and saw a figure charging towards her, waving his arms.

'What the hell are you doing, intruder?' he yelled.

The sight of the man filled Morwenna with fright and she fled towards the mirror. She sped at full pace across the lawn. Just before reaching at her destination, she stumbled over a tree stump and banged her head against the garden bench which was just a few metres from the wall. She fell to the ground and everything went black. As she came to, Morwenna was aware of herself being dragged across the freezing cold ground, by the arm. She fully awoke to the sensation of Titan licking her face. The air was warmer again and she was back in 2020. She sat up and hugged the dog. The right sleeve of the puffer jacket was partially torn away and some fragments were in Titan's mouth. He had traversed the mirror into 1962, when she was knocked unconscious, and he had literally dragged her by the arm, back through the mirror into 2020.

Titan and his mistress helped each other back to the kitchen and she sank into the sofa by the kitchen range, which still exuded some warmth. Gradually she became aware of a pain above her eye and she removed the remains of her coat and tossed it to the floor. The coat was blood stained and torn but her arm was uninjured. Morwenna studied her face in the tarnished antique mirror above the mantlepiece. Although the light was dim, she could see a gash on her head and an advancing black-eye, presumably from striking the garden bench with her head. She hated blood, but she had to bathe the cut on her head as best she could. She found a first aid kit on the shelves behind the kitchen door and extracted a bandage and a bottle of iodine, which looked like a relic from the War. After cleaning the wound and applying the dressing to her head, she revived herself with a cup of sweet tea.

'Well done, Titan, I'll keep you with me for ever.' she said to the dog. 'You are a hero!'

Before retiring to bed, Morwenna opened a tin of dog food and Titan wolfed down his second supper. He knew he had done well.

Chapter 13

The Aftermath

Harriet was awoken by hammering on her door early the next morning. Without waiting for an answer, Ada launched into her bedroom carrying the torn and blood-stained coat and waved it in front of her.

'I found *this* on the floor in the kitchen and the ancient first-aid kit wide open on the table!' shouted Ada looking really concerned. 'The back door was unlocked, even though I'm sure I locked it before I went to bed.'

Harriet leapt out of bed and banged on Morwenna's door with the side of her fist.

'Come in,' advanced a voice from inside.

They barged into the bedroom and Morwenna's dishevelled head slowly emerged from under the quilt. She pushed back her hair and eased herself into a sitting position.

'Oh, my goodness!' screamed Ada as they regarded her face which had a makeshift dressing partly covering a cut on the right side of her forehead. There was some congealed blood above her eye which was swollen and black.

'Had a bit of an accident in the night,' said Morwenna sheepishly.

Harriet asked Ada to go downstairs and return with the new first aid kit. Ada then excused herself, satisfied the patient would be looked after. Once the two women were left alone, Morwenna explained what had happened, as her medical companion cleaned and re-dressed the wound.

'Could you have imagined it and then fainted?' asked Harriet, very sceptical about time travel, 'Titan may have pulled you, by the arm of the jacket, to awaken you?'

'Harri, it was real. I could see and hear everything and the man in the garden could see me!' whispered Morwenna.

All of a sudden, Morwenna sprang from her bed and called for Harriet to follow her.

'What are you doing? Don't you think you should rest?' yelled Harriet.

Morwenna ran down the stairs, two at a time, in her pyjamas with her friend in close pursuit. This type of unruly behaviour was most unlike her. She was usually controlled and disciplined in her actions.

She gesticulated theatrically towards the sitting room, flailing her arms and shouting, 'I know how to prove it. *Love Me Do* by the Beatles!'

The 1960's gramophone stood on the sideboard. Grasping the cabinet door with eagerness, she flung it open and seized the stack of records. She threw to one side; *I Can't Stop Loving You* by Ray Charles and grabbed the record underneath; *Love Me Do* by the Beatles.

'Look it's here and they were playing it last night,' said Morwenna, thrusting the dusty single towards Harriet.

Harriet slid the record from its sleeve and nodded her head slowly, in reluctant affirmation. The name; *Catherine Nicholas* was scrawled across the paper circle in the centre of the single, in her childish hand.

After a few minutes of recovery, Morwenna approached the grandfather clock and noted that the pendulum was not moving. The clock had stopped at eleven o'clock.

'Look Harri,' said Morwenna. 'I've never seen a grandfather clock with a date on before This is really weird. The time on the grandfather clock says eleven and the date reads *28th May 2020*.'

Harriet came to her friend's side and peered at the clockface. After a while, she said, 'It's a little odd to set it for the day before Edith died. I wonder if Ada did that?'

'Maybe she stopped winding it after Edith died?' suggested Morwenna. 'The clock's not ticking and I've never heard it chime since we came here.'

'Interesting, we'll ask Ada about that later,' said Harriet. 'It's also curious that Titan can travel through the mirror to 1962, as well as you.'

'Yes, he did. That's true,' replied Morwenna.

'Anyway, we can remove one suspect from our investigation with absolute certainty,' said Harriet knowingly.

'How is that?' questioned Morwenna.

'Well, we can take the trespasser off the list. It was you!'

'Blimey, yes I never thought of that. I was the middle-aged woman wearing the; *unusual short yellow quilted coat* mentioned in the newspaper article,' replied Morwenna.

'Never liked that coat anyway, glad its ruined,' mused Harriet, looking thoughtful.

'It's not looking good for Jonathan though,' reflected Morwenna. 'Catherine threatened to tell Emily Watson about their relationship. Could Jonathan have killed Catherine to keep her quiet?'

'Possible,' replied Harriet, 'but Catherine didn't die until the early hours of New Year's Day. Even if Jonathan was the killer, which I don't think he was, why wait a week? The delay would have given Catherine seven days to tell Emily their secret, so it makes no sense.'

The two women returned to their respective rooms to dress, and Ada prepared breakfast. Morwenna had a slight headache so she took two paracetamol and vowed to keep going until the mystery was solved. After eating, they returned to the library to plan their interviews for the afternoon. Morwenna had arranged to visit Joseph Penhaligon directly after lunch and her companion was driving to Helston to see Emily Watson.

'Harri, we also need to find out from Ada, who was staying in which bedroom. My room is above the morning room and yours is above the study. Both have good visibility of the south terrace and the railings guarding the cliff. Somebody might have heard something,' proposed Morwenna.

'But it would have been dark,' replied her friend.

'The lights from the drive illuminate the south terrace at night,' explained Morwenna.

'We need to check whether those lights were there in 1962, and if they were left on,' said Harriet thoughtfully.

Harriet sketched a diagram of the house, both downstairs and upstairs and Ada helped them fill it in. Back in 1962, Edith occupied her current bedroom above the sitting room and overlooking the lawned gardens and summer house, to the north of Gwedr Iowarth. Over Christmas and New Year in 1962, Frank and Mavis Nancarrow had been staying in Harriet's room (above the study) and Jonathan was lodging in Morwenna's room (above the morning room). So potentially Frank, Mavis or Jonathan could have witnessed the events which occurred on the south terrace, depending at what time they went to bed.

Anyone could have accessed the study or morning room, both of which, faced the south terrace. Ada confirmed that the drive was illuminated by electric lights in 1962. These were left on because some of the guests were leaving by car, after the party. The switch for the drive lights was located in the kitchen and she had left them on deliberately, that night. The lights were not extinguished until the following morning.

'I leave the drive lights on most of the time, nowadays,' said Ada, 'for security, you see. But in those days the lights were only lit, if we had guests.'

Ada couldn't account for the movements of any of the suspects after she went to bed at ten o'clock on the night of the murder and she reported hearing nothing untoward.

'I never hear much from my room, because it's on the top floor and overlooks the kitchen garden,' said Ada. 'But I do remember that Dr Watson and Emily didn't stay overnight at Gwedr Iowarth. They went home by car. Phillipe Bouvier also left in his own vehicle. Morgan and Ebrel were in the bedroom over the library and Catherine slept in her own room, the one over the dining room, next to Edith's.'

'When was the grandfather clock last wound?' Harriet asked Ada.

'It stopped working in January 1963 and never went again after Catherine died. The winding mechanism is completely jammed,' said Ada. 'Miss Nancarrow was so upset after Catherine died that she didn't deal with anything. The housekeeper called a clocksmith to service the mechanism and set it going again.'

'What happened?' asked Morwenna.

'The clocksmith said the mechanism was totally seized up and would need to be replaced at quite a high cost,' replied Ada. 'Miss Nancarrow said the chimes kept her awake so she refused to have it mended, and that was that.'

'The date on the clock says *28th May 2020*. That was the day before Edith died,' said Morwenna.

'I've not touched that clock since 1963 except to polish the case,' said Ada springing up and heading out of the library towards the sitting room.

Morwenna and Harriet followed Ada into the sitting room and the housekeeper made a beeline for the clock. The three of them crowded around Ada, who looked at the face and date dial quizzically. She crossed the room to the sideboard and opened the cupboard to the right of the drawers. Her hand moved to a gap above the top shelf, and she revealed a *secret drawer*. She extracted a ring containing two keys. Ada crossed back to the clock and used one key to open the lock on the glass door and she looked closely at the dials. Ada attempted to move the dials next to the date display and concluded that they remained jammed.

'The time and date on that clock have not changed in the last fifty years. I don't think anyone has touched it since 1963. I have the vaguest memory of Miss Nancarrow saying that the date dial had *gone mad and set itself to 2020* and the clock couldn't be wound,' explained Ada. 'You used to be able to change the date by moving the dials to the side of each number on the date display. I had to do it a few times before Catherine died if the former housekeeper had let the clock stop.'

'I don't like coincidences,' said Harriet. 'The clock stopped soon after Catherine died in 1963. The date dial miraculously changed to the evening before Edith's death and remained like that for nearly fifty years. It's weird, really weird.'

'Does anyone else know where the clock keys are kept?' asked Morwenna.

'No one who's alive,' said Ada, 'and I don't think the date dial has been changed. I'm pretty sure the date May 2020 has been there since Catherine died.'

Morwenna and Harriet spent the next couple of hours refining the questions they had for Emily Watson and Joseph Penhaligon and after lunch they went their separate ways.

Chapter 14

Emily Watson

Harriet climbed into her car and Morwenna waved her off.

'Try and be discreet,' yelled Morwenna through the car window, but her futile words were drowned by the din of the car engine. A flurry of dust generated by Harriet's wheels rose from the shale drive as she sped off.

Harriet covered the short distance to Helston to visit Miss Emily Watson in under ten minutes. Her destination was on the outskirts of the town. *Le Bois* was a symmetrical Georgian house of granite with traditional casement windows. To the left of the property was a small wood, which presumably gave the house its name. On the right was a stony farm lane, meandering into the distance. The iron gates, with their spiked finials, had been set open to allow Harriet easy access. It was a warm day and Harriet had been instructed to park at the front, and proceed on foot through the side gate into the back garden. She paused for a moment in the car, while she planned to adapt her narrative to exclude the fact that Jonathan Coutts was now married to Morwenna. Harriet didn't want any emotional memories to distract Emily Watson from recalling the factual events surrounding Catherine's death.

When Harriet arrived at the back of the house, her informant was already sitting in the garden and she rose to meet her with a nod and a friendly smile. Emily gestured for her visitor to take a seat.

'Nice to meet you Mrs Duncan. I thought we would be better outside, because of COVID.'

'Of course, thanks for letting me come. Please call me Harriet.'

'Call me Emily,' Miss Watson replied. 'I'll make us some tea and then you can tell me what this is all about. How do you take it?'

'Milk, no sugar,' replied the visitor.

Emily returned after a few minutes, with tea and cake laid out on a tray. Harriet had already calculated that she was seventy-eight years old and had been twenty-one at the time of Catherine's death. Her host was small and quite stocky, although not overweight. Her grey hair was very short and she was wearing jeans, a colourful shirt and punkish black boots. Harriet had not been expecting that.

Emily possessed a temperate but frank disposition and certainly did not appear to be a likely candidate for a murderer. Harriet tried to assess her chances of being able to push Catherine over the railings. She concluded it was possible, if she had an element of surprise, but only because the railings were significantly lower in 1962 than they were now. She made an abrupt decision simply *to come clean* with Emily and tell her the truth. Harriet suspected her host was a no-nonsense sort of person and would not be taken in by Harriet, if she tried too much deception. However, Harriet did not intend to mention Morwenna's connection with Jonathan as that may unsettle her.

'I'm staying at *Gwedr Iowarth*,' started Harriet, 'with my good friend Morwenna who has recently inherited the property and estate from Miss Edith Nancarrow, her great aunt.'

'Of course, I saw the notice of her death in the Newspaper. I'd not seen Edith for many years. We didn't keep in contact after my father died.'

'I'm not sure if you are aware but Morwenna is the daughter of Morgan and Ebrel Trevethan. For personal reasons it has become necessary for her to try and get to the bottom of Catherine Nicholas' death,' said Harriet.

'I was intrigued when you called and I guessed it must have been something to do with Catherine,' replied Emily, 'I'll help you if I can, although the police did a pretty thorough investigation at the time.'

'What do you recall about the New Year's Eve party in 1962?' asked Harriet, thinking it was better to start with a fairly open-ended question.

Emily explained that she was living with her father Dr Frederick Watson at *Le Bois*. They had been invited to the New Year's Eve party several weeks before and they had arrived for a buffet-supper at about seven-thirty. The party had taken place across the dining-room, sitting-room and hall, although people could also move in and out of the kitchen if they wished. Apparently, Jonathan and Phillipe had carried the gramophone into the hall which was favoured for dancing, as it contained less furniture. The only other room in regular use was the cloakroom, by the front door.

'Most people smoked in those days,' said Emily, 'and they usually lit-up outside the front door because Edith wouldn't let people smoke indoors.'

'What time did people leave?' asked Harriet.

'The first person to go was Mavis Nancarrow. She complained of a headache and left the party before midnight. She was staying at the house, of course, so she just went upstairs.'

'What was her behaviour and manner like that evening?' enquired Harriet.

'She was fine. I didn't know Mavis that well, but she seemed to be relaxed and enjoying the party. She was quite a beauty, Mavis, a bit loud but fun to have at a party. I guess she would have been in her fifties but she was still quite *with it*!' expanded Emily.

'Who left next?' questioned Harriet, who was scribbling notes while listening intently to her host.

'Well, that was Catherine,' said Emily. 'Normally she would have been the last in bed, but her foot was terribly swollen and painful. She had cut it, whilst out walking, the previous day. My father was called to attend to her injury. He also examined her at the beginning of the party and said everything was fine. He reminded her not to weight bear for long and, she wasn't to dance.'

'What time did Catherine go?' asked Harriet.

'She went up at about twelve thirty and I didn't see her after that,' said Emily. 'In fact, that was the last time I *ever* saw her. It was the last time anyone saw her alive. Apparently, no one checked on her after that and her disappearance wasn't noticed until the next day when she didn't come down to breakfast.'

'How could Catherine have accessed the south terrace without being seen, if people were in the hall?' asked Harriet.

'Easy,' said Emily, 'she must have come down the back-stairs to the kitchen and then out of the kitchen door.'

'Of course,' said Harriet, noting Emily and probably the other guests obviously knew about the back-stairs.

'Why would she have gone to the terrace?' enquired Harriet.

'No one knows for sure,' replied Emily. 'Maybe to meet someone or just to think. I suppose she could have been forced to go there. It was very cold and snowy on that night, so she must have gone there for a reason, I would have thought.'

'Who could have met her?' asked Harriet.

'I've thought about this a lot over the years,' said Emily. 'Anyone could have slipped away from the party to access the south terrace. They could have left through the front door or the French windows in the sitting room or dining room. In reality, you wouldn't miss someone for a few minutes. Those who had retired to bed could have slipped down the back-stairs and out of the kitchen door.'

'Who was the next to leave the party?' asked Harriet.

'Jonathan retired to bed at about quarter to one and Phillipe departed by car at about one o'clock in the morning. I actually saw him drive away. My father and I chatted at the front door with Edith for about fifteen minutes and then we drove away at about quarter past one,' replied Emily.

'What about Ebrel and Morgan Trevethan?' asked Harriet.

'They were quite wrapped up in each other, newly-weds. I think they'd only married in the summer of '62. I presume they went to bed after I left or while we were chatting by the front door.'

'Do you think Ebrel and Morgan Trevethan or Mavis and Frank Nancarrow would have had any reason to kill Catherine?' asked Harriet.

'None at all,' replied Emily. 'They seemed to get on quite well. I was informed that Frank and Mavis Nancarrow were bitter about Edith having all the money and the house, but they had no reason to harm Catherine. They believed everything had been left to the family. To be truthful it would have made more sense for them to kill Edith, if they were going to kill *anyone* for money.'

'So, they didn't know about Edith's will leaving everything to Catherine?' asked Harriet.

'Absolutely not. No one did. That only came out *after* Catherine died. The police quizzed my father about it because he was close to Edith. Even he was unaware about the will bequeathing the estate to Catherine. In fact, my father overheard Mavis Nancarrow reminding her husband that they needed to keep on good terms with Edith. This would ensure Frank and Mavis or more likely their daughter, Ebrel would inherit everything when Edith died,' explained Emily.

'When did your father hear that conversation?' asked Harriet.

'Oh, just a few days before Catherine died,' said Emily. 'My father was washing his hands in the cloakroom with the door open and they were talking in the hall. I understand they were always short of money and they relied on Edith sending them a monthly cheque.'

'What was the relationship like between Frank and Mavis and their daughter Ebrel?' asked Harriet.

'Mavis doted on Ebrel. She was her only surviving child, of course. Apparently, Mavis had quite a few miscarriages. During the War, Mavis and Frank were staying at Gwedr Iowarth and my father was called to attend Mavis after losing another baby,' explained Emily.

'What else do you remember of the police investigation?' asked Harriet.

'It was awful. The police really grilled me, Jonathan, Phillipe and my father,' said Emily.

'Why?' asked Harriet.

'Jonathan was engaged to me, but he fancied Catherine. They had a bit of a *fling,* as we called it in those days. No sex of course, just a bit of snogging. Jonathan didn't think I knew, although, I had suspected it for a while. On Christmas Eve, we young ones were together: me, Catherine, Jonathan and Phillipe. We had a Christmas celebration at Gwedr Iowarth. Phillipe and I left the sitting room to go for fresh drinks, but I told Phillipe I could manage on my own, so he remained in the hall. He spotted them kissing through the sitting room door which was ajar. He then proceeded to the kitchen and told me what he'd seen,' explained Emily.

'What did you do?' asked Harriet.

'I said nothing at the time. I needed time to think. I did tell my father and he was *furious* with Jonathan and Catherine. To be honest I was relieved, as I was planning to break things of with Jonathan in the New Year, so I persuaded my father to leave things alone. I was far too young to marry and I wanted the chance to train as a teacher,' said Emily.

'What did the police think?' asked Harriet.

'Well, they thought we all had motives to harm Catherine. My motive was anger and jealousy that my fiancé was having a relationship with Catherine. Jonathan admitted that Catherine had threatened to tell me about his relationship with Catherine. He had to admit that, because Phillipe had overheard the conversation on Christmas Eve. So, Jonathan's motive was to silence Catherine by killing her. My father's alleged motive was his anger at Catherine for upsetting me. Finally, Phillipe was very attracted to Catherine and he had overheard her tell Jonathan that she wasn't interested in him, so the police say he could have felt *rejected*,' explained Emily.

'What was Phillipe like,' asked Harriet.

'He adored the sound of his own voice,' answered Emily. 'He was older than Catherine, Jonathan and I and he liked to present himself as sophisticated and experienced. I guess he viewed himself as *a man of the world*! We were impressed in the beginning, of course, especially because he was from abroad.'

'Did Phillipe ever become angry?' asked Harriet.

'He was the only one of us with a bad temper. It didn't take much to make him flare-up. But in truth, I don't think he or any of us younger ones were involved in harming Catherine and certainly not my father,' said Emily.

'Can you be sure about your father? Parents can be very protective,' Harriet pointed out.

'Honestly he did not have an aggressive bone in his body,' explained Emily. 'My mother died in childbirth with me. So, 6th March 1942 was the day I was born and the day my mother died. We were very close because there was just the two of us. After Catherine died, I broke things off with Jonathan and went to train as a teacher. Best thing I ever did.'

'Did you ever see your father become angry?' asked Harriet.

'Rarely,' replied Emily. 'He was almost blind in one eye and he sometimes became frustrated about that. It had hampered his career. It stopped him being posted to Europe during the War and prevented a vocation for surgery. But generally, he was mild-mannered and accepted life as it was.'

'I understand you never married,' reflected Harriet, hoping she was not pushing Emily too hard.

'I didn't. Teaching was my life. After I qualified as a teacher at Bingley Teacher Training College, I worked in Kenya for a while and then came back to a girls' school in Truro,' said Emily.

'Did you meet anyone else?' pressed Harriet.

'I did,' expressed Emily with a radiant smile. Her expression of pleasure waned to a wistful look. 'I met the love of my life, another teacher at Truro School. We were together for over forty years. She died eighteen months ago.'

'She?' asked Harriet before she could stop herself.

'Yes,' said Emily. 'That was one of the reasons I had to split up with Jonathan. I realised I didn't fancy men! I kept Helen a secret from my father, but she moved in with me here, after he died.'

'You mentioned Phillipe had a temper,' said Harriet. 'What made you say that?'

'Small things. If he was criticised or teased, he could become very angry. One time we were playing tennis at Gwedr Iowarth and he flung his racquet at Jonathan and accused him of making a bad call,' remembered Emily. 'Mind you, it was a really hot day.'

'How did Jonathan react?' asked Harriet.

'He was a bit taken aback but he calmed the situation down and Phillipe soon apologised,' replied Emily. 'Then we went swimming to cool off, although Catherine didn't come in the water. She never did.'

'Why did Catherine not swim?' asked Harriet.

'She said she couldn't swim because they never taught them in the children's home. I don't think that was true. I think she was frightened of the sea because she wouldn't even take her shoes off and have a little paddle in the water!'

'Was she frightened of heights?' asked Harriet.

'No, I don't think so. She liked to walk on the cliffs and there are some pretty terrifying drops around here,' pointed out Emily.

'What happened to Phillipe after Catherine's death?' asked Harriet.

'He went to America, I think,' explained Emily. 'Things soured for us all I guess, and we went our separate ways. Phillipe to America, me to Bingley and Jonathan was transferred to London. Shall we have a stroll around my garden Harriet?'

Emily and Harriet walked around the beautifully kept grounds. Emily explained that the garden was in the best shape because she had spent so much time there during lock-down. They paused to admire one of the rose-beds and Harriet remembered to ask about Ada.

'Do you remember Ada Bray?' enquired Harriet.

'Yes, of course. I see her from time to time in Helston and Falmouth. I saw her in a few plays shown by Falmouth Amateur Dramatics Society. I used to enjoy acting and producing myself when I was a teacher. We put on quite a lot of productions at the school.'

'How was Ada's relationship with Catherine?' asked Harriet.

'Not sure really,' said Emily. 'They had both come from Helston Children's home but there was quite an age gap. Ada was about fifteen and Catherine twenty when Catherine died. There didn't appear to be any closeness or warmth between them, nor any animosity, from what I can remember anyway.'

'Could Ada have been envious of Catherine's position in the house?' asked Harriet.

'Looking back on things, it must have been difficult for Ada,' reflected Emily. 'Catherine was Edith's ward and companion. Edith treated her like a member of the family. My father said Edith let Catherine get away with *far* too much. Ada, on the other hand, was a servant. She lived on the top floor and she didn't mix with the family socially. It was the way of things at the time, but it seems awful now.'

'Do you think Ada could have killed Catherine?' asked Harriet.

'It is logistically possible. Ada could have come down the back-stairs and left by the kitchen door,' said Emily thoughtfully. 'But why would she be meeting Catherine on the terrace in the early hours of the morning?'

'I see what you mean. That does seem a bit far-fetched,' agreed Harriet as they emerged around the side of Emily's house.

Emily led her visitor back to her car and Harriet sensed their discussion was being drawn to a close. She thanked her host who assured her that Harriet could call her again if she thought of any further questions.

'If you do work out what happened, you will let me know won't you?' said Emily as Harriet opened the car door.

'I will of course, goodbye.'

Harriet left Emily Watson's house with a cheerful heart. Her honesty about love and devotion had touched Harriet. She drove away believing Emily was an unlikely murderer. Alternatively, Emily had put on the most cunning performance Harriet had ever encountered.

Chapter 15

Joseph Penhaligon

While Harriet was visiting Emily Watson, Morwenna called on Joseph Penhaligon at Gwedr Iowarth Cottage. She opened the rickety gate that separated the two properties, having to support its weight to prevent the hinges collapsing. The cottage garden was immaculate with neat rows of vegetable and flower beds.

The interior of the house, on the other hand, was a disaster. The main reception room doubled as a sitting room and kitchen. There was a 1950's dresser with chipped blue paint, a large rough wooden table and two ancient armchairs. The fireplace was open and the remnants of the previous evening's fire still sat in the grate. Every surface was littered with half-used packets of food. The crockery and cutlery were clean but randomly stacked on the dresser and table, interspersed with tools such as screw-drivers and hammers. Faded and tattered blue checked curtains hung at the small window. Morwenna needed no convincing that this property had been occupied by men for the last fifty years with no sign of a woman's touch.

'I know it's a mess,' pleaded Joseph apologetically, seeing Morwenna's eyes roaming around his front room and cringing under her inspection. 'Miss Nancarrow pushed me to let her update it. *Put in central heating and a fitted kitchen*, she said, but I didn't want the bother. Too stressful by far. Err, what happened to your face?'

Morwenna touched her eye and said, 'Oh I tripped over a tree stump, near the garden bench and hit my head.'

'Strange,' retorted Joseph, 'I dug that tree stump out in 1970, after I fell over it myself one night.'

Idiot, Morwenna thought to herself and then said out loud, 'Must have been Titan I tripped over, it *was* dark'.

Joseph let the cause of her black-eye drop and suggested they have a cup of coffee and get down to business. He explained that he had been born and brought up at Gwedr Iowarth and his father, William, had been the head gardener. His mother had died when he was twelve, of cancer. There had just been himself and his father after that, and Joseph had naturally followed his father's footsteps.

'When did you and Catherine first meet?' started Morwenna.

'Catherine came here in, er, 1956. I was fourteen at the time, and she was thirteen.'

'How did she become Edith's ward?' asked Morwenna.

'Goodness I remember it well,' mused Joseph with his hand over his mouth, 'It caused a hell of a stir at the time. Miss Nancarrow's mother died in 1954 and then her father, Jory passed away a couple of years later. No sooner had he been buried, and she moved Catherine here from the children's home.'

'Why did Catherine's move here cause such a reaction?' asked Morwenna.

'Miss Nancarrow had always kept an interest in Helston Children's Home. In those days it was fine for rich young ladies to have charitable inclinations. But, to take an orphan into your home, and remember she was black! Don't forget the racism in the 1950's. It was a very different time from now.'

'What did Frank and Mavis Nancarrow think?' asked Morwenna.

'They never *said* anything to Miss Nancarrow. They needed the allowance from her, of course, but they were very annoyed. As a gardener you overhear things. My father told me he heard them talking about Catherine when she first came here and saying she might steal things or, *murder them in their beds!*' explained Joseph.

'How did you get on with Catherine?' asked Morwenna.

'Really well. When she first came here, we were young enough to play a bit together the first summer. We climbed trees and had picnics. She was fun, wild and quite daring. She wasn't afraid of anything, except water.'

'And later on?' enquired Morwenna.

'Things changed as she grew up. We were always friends but I was the gardener's son and she was really treated like a member of the family. She became quite tall and a real beauty. Most young men were attracted to her and I was no different.'

'Was there anything between you?' asked Morwenna, surprised at her own bluntness.

'Goodness no,' said Joseph tilting his head forwards with slight embarrassment. 'I was shy, really shy and then my illness started. But she was always kind to me even though she was *a bit of a madam* to other people. Her death affected me very badly in many ways.'

'Do you mind telling me about that?' enquired his interrogator, as gently as she could.

'Well, it was in the autumn of 1962 I had my first *episode*,' explained Joseph. 'I was always reserved, an introvert, but I started to be frightened of people and going out. Then the demons started.'

'Demons?' said Morwenna.

'I could hear messages from the telephone wires. It was like voices were being beamed into my bedroom. I put tin foil over the window to stop them. Whispering words, telling me I would be killed. My father called Dr Watson and he gave me pills called tranquillizers. I thought the medication was poison and flushed the tablets down the toilet. Things came to a head on Christmas Eve of 1962. I ran into the grounds of the house to escape the voices and my father came looking for me. That was when he saw the trespasser in the yellow coat and chased her off.'

'I see,' said Morwenna, 'so your father was out looking for *you* that evening.'

'He was petrified I would be put in an asylum if anyone saw me in that state. So, my father shut me in my room and watched me taking the tablets for the next few days. Dr Watson knew what was happening to me and the police forced him tell them everything about my illness, after Catherine died.'

'Did they suspect you?' asked Morwenna.

'Yes,' replied Joseph. 'They said I could have left my room on New Year's Eve and pushed her off the terrace.'

'Surely your father could have confirmed that you were with him?' enquired Morwenna.

'He was quite drunk that night. He didn't usually take alcohol but he had been given a bottle of whiskey for Christmas and he was under a lot of stress because of my illness. I think I was, *out of it,* on a high dose of medication. Dr Watson had given me an injection that morning, so I couldn't remember much about New Year's Eve,' explained Joseph.

'What do *you* think happened to Catherine?' asked Morwenna.

'Well, she didn't just fall on her own,' stated Joseph, 'and I really can't see her killing herself deliberately. I think she was pushed. Maybe Jonathan Coutts did it to keep Catherine quiet about their relationship. Maybe the family were jealous of Catherine being Edith's ward. I wonder if the family had found out about Miss Nancarrow's will, leaving the house and money to Catherine? The problem is everyone had a motive with the exception of Miss Nancarrow herself and my father.'

'How was her body discovered?' asked his visitor.

'Catherine didn't come down to breakfast on New Year's Day. They left her for a while as they all had a late night. But about ten o'clock, Miss Nancarrow went to her room. Her bed had not been slept in. Everyone, except me, started searching. My father discovered her, with her head smashed on the rocks, below the south terrace.'

Joseph explained that he had become so mentally unwell he had been sectioned and admitted to hospital, soon after Catherine's death. His father had told him about the reactions of the family and friends.

'Miss Nancarrow was the most affected. She was distraught. At first the police made everyone stay locally for a few weeks. But once the police had finished interviewing them all, she asked them all to leave and *never come back*. She suspected every single one of them of having a hand in Catherine's death. She even hired a private investigator but they could never prove anything. So, the murderer escaped scot free.

I heard Miss Nancarrow tell her solicitor, in the garden, to stop all payments to Frank and Mavis Nancarrow. After Frank, Mavis, Ebrel and Morgan left, we never saw them again.'

'Did Edith suspect you?' asked Morwenna.

'I really don't think so. She kept me on here after my father died,' said Joseph. 'She always treated me very well.'

'What about Emily Watson?' asked Morwenna.

'She's pretty low on my list of suspects. I wondered about her at the time but she broke up with Jonathan after Catherine died. If she had killed Catherine to keep Jonathan for herself, that wouldn't have made any sense,' replied Joseph.

'How about my parents, Ebrel and Morgan Trevethan?' enquired Morwenna.

'They had only recently married, so that was the first time I met your father. They seemed very taken with each other. Now we know Miss Nancarrow had left everything to Catherine, Ebrel and Morgan would have had the strongest financial motive to kill Catherine. When you think about it, Frank and Mavis Nancarrow were older than Edith, so they were likely to die before her and never inherit. But actually, Ebrel and Morgan were years younger than Edith. But they thought the will had left everything to the family, so it would have made more sense to kill Edith. Why kill, Catherine?'

'Perhaps Ebrel and Morgan had found out about the will?' suggested Morwenna.

'I don't think so. Apparently, the only copy of the will was kept with the solicitor and it was never accessed by anyone else,' replied Joseph. 'The police were particularly thorough about that. My father said they searched the solicitor's office and interviewed his staff!'

'Yes,' said Morwenna, thinking it could be useful to have another look at the will and see who witnessed it.

'So, you see why Miss Nancarrow had to give up investigating this. I don't think you'll get much further,' said Joseph. 'I'm sorry to change the subject but can I ask about the cottage. I know it's scruffy but I don't want to leave. Will I be able to stay?'

'Yes. Yes of course,' replied Morwenna with a smile. 'I've decided to have the deeds transferred over to you. I'll telephone the solicitor and sort that out. I certainly don't need the cottage! But you will be my neighbour because I've decided to stay at Gwedr Iowarth.'

'You're going to *give* the cottage to me?' asked Joseph grinning from ear to ear.

'Yes,' replied Morwenna.

'Sorry, just one more thing before I go. How easy would it have been to push someone over the railings? You told us Edith had much higher ones put in after Catherine's death,' asked Morwenna.

'Well, I am six foot tall so the railings would only have come up to my hip. You are much smaller so the railings would have been waist-height against you. Catherine was pretty tall. I would say, about five foot nine. I think any adult could have done it, especially if she was not expecting the push. She was also a bit incapacitated by her foot injury and she had taken a few drinks.'

'Was Catherine prone to wandering in the grounds at night in the dark?' asked Morwenna.

'No definitely not,' said Joseph. 'Catherine must have had a reason to be out there at night, she didn't like the cold. Maybe she met with someone on the terrace? The police thought that too and they specifically asked Jonathan Coutts and Phillipe Bouvier if they had arranged to meet her. They both denied it.'

'What was Phillipe Bouvier like?' asked Morwenna.

'Arrogant, didn't like him at all,' answered Joseph with a frown. 'He was a few years older than Catherine and he sort of strutted around the place, as if he was really important. He taught at the school and they didn't like him there either. I heard he was dismissed from Porthleven Council school.'

'Why?' asked Morwenna.

'Not sure,' replied Joseph. 'Maybe they knew he was a murder suspect and couldn't trust him. Anyway, he was gone within a few weeks of Catherine's death and never been heard of since.'

Morwenna made a mental note to look further into Phillipe Bouvier's background and decided to call it a day with Joseph as her head was aching. Joseph was delighted about the cottage and as she left him, he was sitting contently on his front step, smoking a cigarette. Morwenna strolled back to the house and waited for Harriet.

Chapter 16

Information Gathering

By four o'clock in the afternoon, Morwenna and Harriet were sitting on the south terrace exchanging notes about their respective meetings and enjoying a few rays of sunshine. The sun had moved to the west, casting beams of light onto the sea which had become increasingly lively as the afternoon progressed. Harriet had carried the blackboards outside and she was updating the information about each suspect and their motives and opportunities to kill Catherine.

'Who are your top suspects?' Harriet asked her friend.

'I'd like to say Phillipe Bouvier but, in truth, Jonathan and my parents seemed to have the most incentive. Although we have no evidence my parents knew about the will,' replied Morwenna.

'Perhaps Ebrel and Morgan started to see how close Edith was to Catherine and just wanted to get her out of the way to leave their way clear to inherit later on?' proposed Harriet.

'How well do you remember my parents?' asked Morwenna.

'Pretty well. In those days we called other people's parents, Mr and Mrs, do you remember? I always called them, Mr and Mrs Trevethan. That would be unheard of now!' laughed Harriet. 'They both seemed very calm and even-tempered. I certainly can't imagine them killing anyone.'

'My father had a pretty good job and they weren't short of money later on, but as newly-weds they had nothing, so that's a possible motivator to kill Catherine. Also, my grandparents were definitely short of money and quite bitter that they had to accept hand-outs from Edith. Because of that, they couldn't help my parents financially,' reflected Morwenna.

'But could your parents have been killers? Did they have the temperament for it?' asked Harriet.

'I guess anyone can kill, given the right set of circumstances. I never saw my father lose his temper or become violent, but my mum had a short fuse about certain things. I once saw her kick the washing machine because it wouldn't start,' said Morwenna lamely and gestured the palms of her hands upwards.

'A far cry from cold-blooded murder, Wenna,' Harriet replied.

'But we keep coming back to the fact that the family were unaware of the will leaving everything to Catherine. If they truly believed the family would inherit, as Edith had inferred to them, they would have killed Edith, wouldn't they?' said Harriet.

Morwenna and Harriet needed more information. They decided to conduct some further research about Phillipe Bouvier, his temper and why he was sacked from his job as a school teacher and look at Edith's will to Catherine. They also planned to look through some of the older files and diaries to see if information about previous events could help.

'It's starting to become chilly and the wind is picking up,' said Morwenna as one of the blackboards nearly blew over. 'Let's go inside and see what we can find before dinner.'

'That's another thing we need to check,' said Harriet. 'The weather conditions on the night Catherine died, to exclude the possibility of her being blown over the railings.'

As they were picking up the blackboards, Ada came up the drive with a spring in her step.

'I've been to my house and the workmen are doing a great job with the new kitchen. A brand-new fitted kitchen, can you imagine! How are you progressing with your investigation? Ada asked. 'Are you ready to interview me yet?'

'Oh, I'm glad you offered. I felt a bit awkward asking you,' said Morwenna. 'How about tomorrow?'

'Perfect, tomorrow is fine. Maybe straight after breakfast. I'll go and start supper. It'll be ready at seven!' called Ada as she headed around the back of the house.

'Well, she seems in a good mood,' said Harriet. 'She doesn't seem like a guilty woman! I think Ada was secretive before we found out Catherine had died to protect us, and later when she realised Jonathan had been here in 1963. I think she was worried about you finding out.'

'True, but her behaviour could be a double bluff,' mused Morwenna. 'Perhaps she wanted Catherine out of the way to take her place as Edith's companion? After all she has had a job for life and a free house out of this.'

'Yes, good point. We can't exclude anyone,' said Harriet. 'In fact, we can't even exclude you!'

'What on earth do you mean Harri?' said Morwenna.

'Well, you're the time traveller. You know the will was made out to Catherine. You could travel back in time and kill Catherine to make sure *you* inherit later on!' said Harriet laughing.

'Look I know you're joking Harri, but I could go back to see who *did* kill Catherine,' said Morwenna.

'But how would you time when to travel through the mirror?' asked Harriet.

'Easy,' replied Morwenna, 'time in 1962, is tied to time here, possibly via the grandfather clock. Remember my watch synchronised with the grandfather clock in 1962. I went through the mirror on Christmas Eve. I just return one week later and it will be New Year's Eve.'

'Would you do that?' enquired Harriet. 'It could be dangerous. Remember what happened last time.'

'I'll do it if I have to. If we can't exclude Jonathan as the murderer, I'll have to risk it,' said Morwenna. 'But if we can prove his innocence, I don't think I would.'

'Wenna, you can't stand the sight of blood. How on earth will you watch a murder, without passing out?' whispered Harriet.

'I'll have to deal with it,' replied Morwenna stoically, 'but I must see this through and going back may be the only option.'

'Well let's hope not,' concluded Harriet looking quite alarmed.

The two sleuths set off back to the library, each carrying one of the blackboards. After replacing the blackboards at the end of the library table, Morwenna phoned the solicitor's office and left a message for Angela Smalley to give her a call about Edith's will in relation to Catherine Nicholas. Harriet then set to work, looking through the documents left by Angela Smalley and Morwenna conducted some further research on Phillipe Bouvier via the internet. Harriet quickly located the will Edith had made in favour of Catherine Angela Nicholas. The will was dated 15th May 1957, when Catherine was fourteen years old and living at Gwedr Iowarth. Catherine was the sole recipient and the inheritance would be held in trust until Catherine was twenty-one years old.

'I've found the will,' said Harriet to Morwenna.

'Who signed it?' asked Morwenna?

'Albert Gladstone Smalley, presumably Angela Smalley's grandfather and Jean Alice Evans. We don't have any information on Jean Evans, do we?' replied Harriet.

'Is it possible that Jean Evans told one of Edith's family about that will?' considered Morwenna.

'But Catherine was killed over five years after the will was drawn up. If Jean Evans leaked the information or gossiped about it, why would one of the Nancarrow or Trevethan family members wait five years to kill Catherine?' reflected Harriet.

'Who was the trustee?' asked Morwenna

'Albert Gladstone Smalley or the lead solicitor of Kendal-Smalley Solicitors if Albert Smalley could not undertake the duty,' Harriet read aloud.

'It looks like Edith *knew* she couldn't rely on her family around Catherine, doesn't it?' said Morwenna. 'If she had faith in her family, one of them would have been a trustee.'

At that moment the phone rang and Morwenna went to pick it up.

'Ah, thanks for getting back to me so quickly Angela,' said Morwenna explaining about Jean Evans witnessing the will and asking whether she might have leaked information either deliberately to the family of inadvertently as gossip.

Angela told her that Miss Jean Evans had been the senior legal secretary working at Kendal-Smalley Solicitors from the mid 1950s until the 1980s. She explained that Miss Evans was totally trustworthy and her father would have *bet his life* against her honesty. Although the prospect of Jean Evans leaking information appeared extremely unlikely, Angela promised to check with her father to see if this line of enquiry had been considered at the time.

'Another dead end there, I think,' mused Morwenna and went back to her computer.

The two women decided to focus on Phillipe Bouvier until dinner. Morwenna returned to her genealogy site and managed to ascertain that he had died in 2010 in Milwaukee, USA. She reviewed the Canadian and USA criminal trials registers concentrating the search on Montreal where he was born and brought up and Milwaukee where Phillipe had lived after leaving England in 1963.

'I've found something here,' she said. 'Montreal, Court of Quebec, criminal division, 21st October 1961. Phillipe Louis Bouvier, school teacher of 66 Avenue Perksworth, convicted of *simple assault* (of girl-friend) and sentenced to a fine of twenty dollars and referral to the Quebec Teachers' Licencing Authority.'

'Well that definitely pushes Phillipe Bouvier up our list of suspects. He has *form* for assaulting women and remember he threw a tennis racket at Jonathan,' said Harriet as she added this evidence to the blackboard. 'I bet that's why he came to England in the first place, if he wasn't allowed to teach in Canada and then when he left here, he had to emigrate to America to work. That history looks very suspicious to me.'

The two companions continued their research for a while but there was no evidence that Phillipe had committed any other criminal offences and they couldn't find any newspaper articles about him. Morwenna discovered he had married while living in Milwaukee in 1966 and had a couple of children but the marriage had ended in divorce only a few years later.

Ada put her head around the door, 'Well, you two sleuths. Dinner will be ready in fifteen minutes!'

'Thanks Ada,' they replied in unison and they both marched upstairs to get ready.

Ada treated the women to fresh salmon and new potatoes, which she had bought earlier that day in Falmouth.

'Blimey this food is fantastic,' said Harriet. 'The creamy sauce on the salmon is really tasty.'

'I agree, Ada's cooking is making me put on weight. Jonathan won't recognise me when he returns home. By the way, I tried to call him on his mobile before dinner,' revealed Morwenna, 'got his answer phone again, so I rang his daughter.'

'What did you say to her?' asked Harriet.

'Well, I could hardly say, *I think your father might be a murderer*,' replied Morwenna. 'So, I asked if she had heard from Jonathan and Tim. She said they hadn't but that was normal, and apparently Tim has a satellite phone but they would only set it up in an emergency. We're not likely to have word from them for at least another week.'

'OK so let's hope we've solved it by then!' said Harriet trying to sound optimistic.

The pudding was lemon and meringue pie and Morwenna said, 'I've not had this since the 1970s and it's great.'

After dinner Angela Smalley phoned back and informed them that the police had interviewed everyone in the solicitor's office, including Jean Evans and her grandfather in January 1963. Apparently, the police had declared that their security was water-tight. Only Albert Smalley and his legal secretary, Jean Evans, had seen the will and it was locked in the company safe, for which only Albert and Jean had the combination. So, it had to be assumed that members of Edith's family could not have known the contents.

'Let's call it a day,' suggested Morwenna.

'It's still light and the wind has dropped. Do you fancy walking down to the cemetery to look at Catherine's grave?' suggested Harriet. 'The headstone might provide more information and Edith did tell us to visit.'

'Great idea, come on Titan, walkies!' shouted Morwenna.

Titan sprung up and wagged his tail. He was always keen to take a walk with his mistress. She and Harriet exited the house via the kitchen, collecting Titan's lead en route. Ada was loading the dishwasher.

'Fabulous supper, Ada,' Harriet said and Morwenna smiled in agreement.

Ada acknowledged the praise with a nod of her head and said, 'after I leave, you're going to need some help here. You could put an advert in *The Lady*. Joseph's not getting any younger and he still has periods of illness when he struggles to work. So, you may need to look for a local gardener as well!'

'Joseph seems fine at the moment,' said Morwenna.

'He is very well right now,' explained the housekeeper. 'You'll know when things aren't OK.'

'How?'

'He stays indoors and won't talk. Sometimes he really neglects himself. He can't work when he's like that and the garden quickly becomes unmanageable.'

'What's the best way to help, when that happens?' asked Morwenna.

'Well. Make sure he's taking his meds and, if things are really bad, its best to call his community nurse. I have the number. It's been quite a responsibility for me as well as managing such a large house,' reflected Ada.

'You're right. My goodness you've earned your retirement working here for all these years. I'll advertise for a cleaner straight away so, at least, you only have the cooking to do for the next few weeks. Then I'll look for some help in the garden.'

'My friend Glenda, from church, has a daughter who lost her job in a hotel because of the pandemic. She's looking for work. Shall I ask her to come up for an interview?'

'Brilliant idea Ada,' replied Morwenna.

Morwenna, Harriet and Titan walked briskly into the centre of Porthleven. The women were much fitter than they had been when they arrived and Harriet's symptoms of long-COVID had completely disappeared. Once they arrived at the harbour, Harriet asked directions to the cemetery. It was a dry, cool and breezy evening and the restaurants around the harbour were utilising outdoor seating because eating inside was still illegal due to the pandemic. Table clothes were fastened down to prevent them blowing away. Hardy customers wore outdoor clothes, but they didn't grumble. They were delighted to be allowed to eat-out at all. It was a strange site in England. During ordinary times, evening diners would have eaten indoors in all but the most exceptionally good weather.

'We should book a table here once a week. It will be fun and also a nice break for Ada,' suggested Harriet.

'Good idea,' said Morwenna. 'We'll book on our way back.'

The cemetery was quite large, so the two women separated to systematically search the rows of graves. Harriet loved graveyards and kept becoming distracted by reading about the people who had died and their ages and inscriptions. It took them about half an hour to find what they were looking for. All the Nancarrow graves were grouped in one area. Hedra and Jory Nancarrow were buried together and their headstone was engraved with the dates of their deaths in 1954 and 1956 respectively. Close by, was Catherine's grave, marked Catherine Angela Nicholas, 24th December 1943 to 1st January 1963. Her headstone was just as grand as the one for Hedra and Jory. Catherine's inscription said- *Much loved by Edith Nancarrow and taken long before her time. May those who were responsible find no joy in this life or the next.'*

'Gosh, Edith didn't mince her words,' stated Harriet.

'No real clues there,' said Morwenna, 'except the headstone is very expensive and the reference to *those* who were responsible for her death,'

'Catherine was obviously very important to Edith. Do you think Edith was suggesting more than one person could have been involved in her murder?' asked Harriet.

'Possibly,' replied Morwenna. 'Look here's Edith's grave. No grass on this one yet and there's just the wooden marker provided by the undertaker. I'll need to have a gravestone ordered and we should bring some flowers. I really wish I had met Edith.'

Morwenna, Harriet and the dog returned to Gwedr Iowarth via the bistro in the harbour and booked a meal for the following evening. Harriet made the reservation because Morwenna's black eye still looked quite alarming. It was dusk when they returned home and settled down on the armchairs in the study to have a glass of port. Before long they both felt like dropping off to sleep, so they went up to bed.

Chapter 17

Ada Bray

The next morning, Morwenna awoke in a heightened state of apprehension. She felt physically all right even though her eye was still black and swollen. She had less than a week to prove Jonathan's innocence or she would have to return to 1962 to witness a murder, and attempt to save her marriage. Her mouth became dry and her stomach churned, as she considered her predicament. She descended the stairs hesitantly, feeling disconnected from her surroundings. It was a comfort that Titan was waiting for her faithfully with his head on the bottom step.

'I'll tell you what Titan. If I have to go back again, I'm taking you with me this time,' she said to the dog, who thumped his tail on the ground in agreement.

'Where are you taking him?' asked Ada who overheard Morwenna talking, as she polished the hall table.

'Oh, just into Truro with me,' said Morwenna.

'I've left a cold breakfast on the dining table. Call me when you're ready for our interview. I've written a few notes and I have a book to show you,' said Ada as she tapped her apron pocket.

Harriet was already sitting at the dining table, eating cornflakes and she glanced up at Morwenna.

'My goodness Morwenna. I don't know what the restaurant staff will think of your black eye tonight? said Harriet. 'I hope they don't think I did it!'

'Well, I'm not missing out,' replied Morwenna. 'I've not been out for a meal since January and I'm really looking forward to our outing tonight.'

Ada came in to clear Harriet's plate and said, 'Natalie, Glenda's daughter, is coming to see you for the cleaning job at three o'clock.'

'Excellent,' replied Morwenna. 'I'm off to Truro this morning to see the solicitor and sign some paper-work, because probate has come through, so Harriet is going to do your interview. Is that OK?'

'Perfect,' said Ada.

Harriet had read, and re-read all their investigation notes that morning. She had a feeling Ada was edging towards telling Morwenna that she was ready to move to her house in Falmouth, so it was important to gather all the information they needed now. Harriet had an hour before she was due to meet with the housekeeper, so she decided to start sorting through the box-files in the study. The first one contained old birth and death certificates and invoices for work on Gwedr Iowarth dating back to the 1920s and 1930s. The second was marked - *The War Years.* Harriet tipped the contents onto the desk and started to sort through them. There was Edith's passport from the 1930s and entry stamps and exit stamps from Switzerland indicating she spent a year there when she was seventeen. Edith's wartime identity card and ration books were next. There were quite a few photographs of Edith wearing dungarees and a headscarf, smiling with some other young girls. Harriet looked on the back of one of the photographs and it was marked, *Land Army Halton, near Lancaster, 1941.*

Next Harriet found a rental agreement for a house in Truro, *42 Carclaws Street.* She leant back in her chair and perused the detail of document. The tenancy was in the name of Edith Nancarrow, 1st July 1943 to 30th June 1944. Harriet ran her eyes down the paperwork until they fell on Edith's signature at the bottom. Beside the tenant's signature, was the name of the financial guarantor. She expected to see the words Jory Nancarrow but she was surprised to see the name, *Frederick Watson.* How odd, Harriet thought to herself, tilting her head to one side. She always had a suspicious mind, and she began to wonder if Edith had been having a romance with Dr Watson during the War.

Why else would he act as guarantor for a house rental? Harriet would have expected Edith's father to have assisted her to rent the house in Truro, if she had needed accommodation during the War.

Harriet reviewed her notes of the interview with Emily Watson. Emily's birthday was 6th March 1942 so Dr Watson would have been a widow for just over a year when the tenancy agreement was signed, so a new relationship was possible. There was nothing else of note so she added the rental agreement to the documents of interest on the table in the dining room. She would show them to Morwenna later on. Harriet headed towards the safe to see if she could look at Edith's diaries for 1943 and 1944, but then remembered that those were amongst the missing ones. Either Edith never wrote diaries for the War years *or* they had been removed. Perhaps she had destroyed them to hide her entries about her liaison with Dr Fred Watson?

As a doctor, Harriet knew that the best way to draw people into an interview was to start them off by talking about their childhood and experiences of growing up, and that's what she intended to do. It was another sunny morning, so Harriet and Ada decided to sit on the terrace. Harriet had the whole morning and she intended to use it. Morwenna left for Truro and Harriet and Ada took a tray of tea outside. It was really warm on the south terrace, so Ada went to fetch the umbrella to stop them being burnt.

'OK Ada,' said Harriet. 'Shall we begin?'

With very little prompting Ada described her childhood. Ada Margaret Bray had been born in February 1947 to Clara Jane Bray. Ada had little memory of her birth mother who had been a single parent in Bristol. Before she was two years old, the welfare authorities had stepped in to remove her from a 'problem mother'. She was initially placed in a large children's home in Bristol and then moved to Helston Children's Home in 1950, when it became clear that her mother would not be able to take her back. She was considered too old for adoption. Ada described the regime at the children's home, which sounded austere to Harriet, but Ada assured her was considered very *modern* at the time. She explained that one child, who was very bright, had even been sent to train as a teacher.

'Do you remember Catherine Nicholas at the children's home?' asked Harriet.

'Oh yes definitely. We were in a different dormitory and classes, of course. Catherine much older than me. But I knew her, she stood out for lots of reasons,' replied Ada.

'Such as?' enquired Harriet.

'To start with she was black. In fact, she was the only black person I knew at that time. She was also quite adventurous and sort of presumptuous,' explained Ada.

'What do you mean?' asked Harriet.

'We were quite well treated in the home, but we were expected to keep our expectations modest. In those times, it was impressed on us that we should be *grateful* for what we had. Well, Catherine was neither modest nor grateful. She spoke about wanting to *be somebody* and have beautiful clothes. A lot of the girls mocked her but she didn't seem to care,' explained Ada. 'She even talked about becoming a pop-star. Of course, the girls ate their words when she went to live with Miss Nancarrow.'

'Did children from the home see her after she was living at Gwedr Iowarth?' asked Harriet.

'Oh yes, lots of times. Miss Nancarrow used to bring Catherine to Helston shopping. One time we were on the way to church and we saw Catherine with Miss Nancarrow and Catherine was wearing a beautiful white fur cape, a fitted dress and high-heals, which was all the rage in the 1960s,' replied Ada.

'Was anyone jealous?' asked Harriet.

'Hell yes,' replied Ada with gusto. 'We had to wear a hideous dark blue, shapeless, check pinafores and brown tights. To say we were envious is an understatement.'

'Could one of the older students or an ex-resident at the children's home have come to find Catherine to kill her? Would feelings of injustice or jealousy be that strong?' enquired Harriet.

'That's the sort of thing a mean person might fantasise about,' reflected Ada, 'but surely not actually do it!'

'So how did Catherine come to be chosen to be Miss Nancarrow's ward?' enquired Harriet.

'I was never told the detail. Miss Nancarrow and Dr Watson were on the board of governors of the children's home. They both took an interest in *all* the children and they had recruited older teenagers to become their employees before. But people like that didn't take orphans into their homes as family members. That sort of thing just wasn't done in those days. Jory Nancarrow, Miss Nancarrow's father was very old-fashioned. He would never have allowed Miss Nancarrow to cross that boundary but after he died in 1956, I guess she could do as she wished,' explained Ada.

'But why Catherine?' asked Harriet.

'I lived in that children's home for over ten years and I noticed one thing,' reflected Ada. 'Attractive children tended to be taken by local families for fostering and adoption. Short, dumpy and plain children, like me, were left behind. People were shocked that Miss Nancarrow took Catherine to live with her. There was a lot of racism in those days. I wasn't surprised though.'

'Why,' asked Harriet.

'The governors always favoured Catherine. She could get away with anything,' explained Ada.

'Like what?' asked Harriet.

'One time a new member of staff started being particularly mean to Catherine. She told Catherine off for being vain and teased her about her curly hair. Within a few weeks, that member of staff was sacked.'

'Really, why was that?' asked Harriet.

'I'm not sure,' replied Ada. 'I have a theory there was something special about Catherine. Maybe that's what led to her being killed?'

'Blimey,' said Harriet. 'Do you think there was some sort of cover-up about her identity?'

'Exactly,' nodded Ada. 'I wasn't there at the time, but one of the ex-residents, Jane Groves, told me that when Catherine was left at Helston Children's Home, she was dropped off in a vehicle! Jane was in one of the front dormitories and she heard a car draw up the night Catherine was abandoned, as a baby.'

'Why was a car unusual?' asked Harriet naively.

'This was during the War, 1943, and at night. Cars were rare. The blackout was on and petrol was scarce. What sort of single mother, having just given birth, would have had a car? Even private car owners could only use cars on official business because of petrol rationing,' whispered Ada.

'What do you think?' asked Harriet.

'I think Catherine Nichols was the daughter of someone high up, a politician maybe or even aristocracy. Illegitimate of course. Maybe the authorities had her killed later, at Gwedr Iowarth, fearing she might have wanted to trace her birth parents and cause a scandal? Remember the trespasser with the yellow quilted coat the week before Catherine died. I say it was all connected,' explained Ada.

'Did the girl, Jane Groves see the driver of the car?' asked Harriet.

'No, there was the blackout rules. But she heard the car door open and close at around the time baby Catherine was left,' said Ada.

'And you Ada, how did it transpire that you came to Gwedr Iowarth?' asked Harriet.

Ada explained that when the boys and girls in the children's home became fifteen or sixteen, they were found jobs, usually with lodgings. Common positions for boys were within the armed services or as apprentices. Girls were often allocated occupations in hotels or as pupil-nurses because these also provided accommodation.

'Going *into service* was becoming much more unusual in the 1960s,' said Ada, 'but the matron of the home was quite fond of me and she knew I loved reading, so when Miss Nancarrow wanted a live-in member of staff, I jumped at it. I was very excited about it because Matron told me there was a library.'

'Did you remain interested in literature?' enquired Harriet, pretending she hadn't seen Ada's book collection.

'Oh yes. I think I've read almost every book in the house and I own a large number of books that I've bought myself,' Ada replied. 'That's the thing I'm most looking forward to in retirement, having unlimited time to read.'

'Did the police interview you after Catherine died?' said Harriet.

'They did and, I must admit, I lied to them,' revealed Ada.

'Really, what did you say?' asked Harriet, edging forward on her seat.

'I told them the truth about going to bed at ten o'clock but I didn't sleep. I read until long after midnight. I honestly had no idea how Catherine came to fall down the cliff but the police asked if I was jealous of her and I said I wasn't. I was frightened they might think I did it. Remember there was still the death penalty for murder back then.'

'How envious were you?' asked Harriet.

'Look, she had everything,' said Ada. 'Catherine was treated like a member of the family. She owned beautiful clothes and didn't have to cook and clean. She was so care-free. She had all day to do as she pleased and I could only do what I wanted, once the housework was done. Catherine had Miss Nancarrow twisted around her little finger. I was fifteen and I wanted someone to be interested in *me* and buy me lovely clothes and ask me about the books I was reading. I wasn't even invited to the New Year party. Catherine never read a book and she wasn't interested in literature.'

'You, say she was disinterested, as far as literature was concerned. What did she enjoy?' asked Harriet. 'What were her talents?'

'Catherine was talented at tennis, although she did have plenty of lessons,' explained Ada. 'Music was probably her best accomplishment. She played the piano and sung very well. Everyone admired her for that. But she soon became bored with things. For example, she would play a little piano and then want to listen to records and dance. Everyone loved her though, whatever she did.'

'Blimey, I would have been jealous. How did *you* feel?' questioned Harriet.

'Furious, I wished Catherine was gone many times. I could have wrung her neck,' admitted the housekeeper, becoming quite irate. Ada's voice then rose to fever pitch. 'She acted like she was in charge, sending me to do errands for her. In my imagination, Miss Nancarrow would have chosen *me* if Catherine wasn't there. Ridiculous really. In all those years, I was never even given permission to call Miss Nancarrow, Edith. We always maintained a staff-employee type of relationship.'

'Did you ever trace your birth mother?' asked Harriet, thinking it was prudent to change the subject.

'I knew her name and she lived in Bristol. I went looking for her in 1970 and I found her with a husband and family. She told me to keep away, because her husband didn't know she'd had an illegitimate child. So that was that,' said Ada, with her palms raised upwards in resignation.

'What do *you* think happened to Catherine?' asked Harriet.

Ada reached into her large apron pocket and pulled out a small book about tracing people's identity through DNA. 'I found this in Falmouth book sellers, it's a very interesting book with lots of information about advances in genetic testing. It seems a bit extreme, but we could exhume her body and have the DNA tested. You can probably trace Catherine's birth families. This could give a clue as to why she was killed.'

'I guess we would need to look at the legal process,' said Harriet who grimaced, rather shocked by Ada's suggestion.

'I've checked that out,' said Ada. 'You would need a court order, so the police would have to re-open the case in the first instance. Also, there could be DNA from the attacker on her clothing, although that would be a longshot so many years later.'

'Changing the subject,' said Harriet. "What did Edith do during the War?'

'She lived away, in Lancashire, I think. She was in the Land Army. Later on, maybe around 1944, Miss Nancarrow worked as a secretary for Major Kent. He was in charge of the Home Guard in Helston so she was back living in Gwedr Iowarth at the end of the War,' explained Ada.

'Did she ever live in a house in Truro?' asked Harriet.

'No, not as far as I'm aware. She never mentioned that,' said Ada. 'Although I wasn't even born then. She quite often talked about the Land Army and working for Major Kent, but she never mentioned Truro.'

'What about Dr Watson. What did he do during the War?' asked Harriet.

'Ah yes Miss Nancarrow did tell me about this. Frederick Watson was a good friend of hers. He was a medical student in London when the war broke out. He had to finish his training even though London was being bombed. He told Miss Nancarrow that part of St Thomas' Hospital was hit while he was in it. Apparently, he was partially blinded in one eye by a blast injury. As soon as he qualified as a doctor, he was called-up but he was posted to Truro Hospital because his wife had died and Emily was a baby. Also, he could only see out of one eye so, the War Office said he couldn't be sent on a foreign posting,' recalled Ada.

'Is it possible he was having a relationship with Edith? I've discovered he acted as a guarantor for a house Edith was renting in Truro in 1943,' explained Harriet.

'It's possible, but why keep it a secret? Dr Watson was a respectable widower and Miss Nancarrow's father wouldn't have objected to Miss Nancarrow forming an attachment to him. He always wanted her to marry. Even after Catherine died, Dr Watson kept visiting here. He was the family doctor but there didn't seem to be anything romantic between them,' said Ada thoughtfully.

'You know Edith always kept a diary,' stated Harriet.

'Yes. She wrote her diary almost daily until Catherine died,' confirmed Ada.

'What about the War years?' asked Harriet. 'They seem to be missing.'

'All the diaries were in the safe, I think,' replied Ada. 'Maybe she was too busy to write diaries in the War?'

'Was it windy on the night Catherine died?' enquired Harriet.

'No, cold and slightly snowy, but no wind,' replied Ada.

The interview came to a natural end. Ada asked Harriet if she thought Morwenna would be all right with her visiting Falmouth that afternoon, seeing as Harriet and Morwenna were eating at a restaurant. Harriet was sure it would be fine and she encouraged Ada to catch an early bus as Harriet would prepare lunch for herself and Morwenna. Ada reminded Harriet that Natalie Fisher was calling at three o'clock to be interviewed for the job as a cleaner and she left to take the bus to Falmouth.

The house seemed strangely empty to Harriet as Morwenna had taken Titan with her to Truro. It appeared that Ada had been very honest and

Harriet thought it highly unlikely that Ada would suggest exhuming Catherine's body, if she had been involved in killing her. On the other hand, she had admitted to being very jealous of Catherine and lying to the police at the time of her death. It must have been difficult for Ada to have to follow orders from Catherine and wait on her when they had both been in the children's home. Surely, envy and burning injustice were powerful motives for murder?

Chapter 18

Out of Lockdown

Morwenna was back by one o'clock. She explained to Harriet that probate had been granted so she was the legal owner of Gwedr Iowarth and she had access to Edith's finances. Harriet had prepared lunch and set it out in the kitchen.

'I don't think Titan is used to travelling by car,' said Morwenna. 'It was a nightmare. He was meant to be lying on the back seat but he barked all the way to Truro and he kept whining and licking the back of my neck. The car rocked as he jumped around.'

'He's probably never been in a car before. Ada doesn't drive and I don't expect Edith would have been driving over the last few years. In any case, your car is totally unsuitable for such a large dog,' replied Harriet. 'You have plenty of money. Why don't you buy a bigger car, like a four-wheel drive or something?'

'That's a good idea. Businesses are opening up again, shall we look at cars this afternoon?' suggested Morwenna.

'That sounds rather hasty for you,' Harriet frowned, in feigned disapproval. 'Anyway, we can't, remember you're interviewing Ada's friend's daughter for the cleaning job.'

'That's true. I got a bit carried away,' replied Morwenna. 'Also, you need to brief me about what Ada said.'

'What's the name of the girl I'm interviewing again?' asked Morwenna

'Natalie Fisher,' replied Harriet. 'I think Ada has set you up there.

She mentioned you would need help after she left and immediately suggested her friend's daughter.'

Over lunch Harriet described Edith's Truro tenancy agreement from 1943 and she summarised the contents of her interview with Ada. Morwenna was surprised to discover how well-informed Ada was about DNA analysis and she was and rather disturbed by the prospect of exhuming Catherine Nicholas' body.

'Let's hope we don't have to dig up the body,' reflected Morwenna. 'I don't really subscribe to the idea that Catherine was the daughter of someone influential. Murders are usually committed by someone within the household. A conspiracy theory doesn't seem very probable and we have no evidence to support it.'

'Is it possible Catherine was related to a well-known or public figure and she was moved to Gwedr Iowarth for her own protection?' suggested Harriet without much conviction her voice.

'It seems a bit far-fetched,' re-iterated Morwenna. 'Eighty percent of murders are committed by friends and family who are in immediate contact with the victim. I read an article about it.'

'If Catherine wasn't biracial,' thought Harriet, out loud, 'I'd be thinking Catherine was the daughter of Edith and Dr Watson.'

'Could she be the daughter of one of them?' mused Morwenna.

'That's more likely than the conspiracy theory, I'll admit. But again, we would have to exhume the body and obtain DNA to find out and it doesn't help us catch the murderer,' said Harriet.

'And, it doesn't help us to clear Jonathan's name, which is my top priority,' replied Morwenna.

'We may have a more immediate issue,' said Harriet, 'I think Ada is keen to make the move to her new house so I think you need to employ Natalie if she's suitable. Oh, and while you're interviewing her, ask her about the murder.'

'She's only in her twenties,' said Morwenna.

'Well, you never know,' replied Harriet optimistically. 'Her mother and grandparents might have lived locally at the time. There are plenty of people who like to gossip in small places like Porthleven. While you interview her, I'm going to search for the lost diaries from the War years, if they exist?'

'It's a worry really,' said Morwenna looking rather forlorn. 'We've interviewed all our living witnesses, except Jonathan, and we are no nearer to identifying the murderer. Let's hope something turns up soon.'

Presently, there was a knock on the back door and Morwenna admitted Natalie Fisher. Harriet introduced herself briefly and left Morwenna and her guest together. Natalie was a petite and boyish young person with elfin features. She had spiky black hair set against her tiny pale face. Her hair was so black, Morwenna believed it was dyed, maybe for gothic effect. She had an expressive face and feline eyes, like a leopard. Her mouth was wide and she had even teeth between full lips.

Natalie greeted Titan excitedly and as she hugged him, Morwenna noticed he was almost as tall as her. Titan characteristically tried to ignore the visitor, as was his usual practice, the first time he met someone. Natalie's speech was articulate, unfussy and to the point. She was confident enough to tease her interrogator gently. But she was also kind and never allowed comedy to give way to rudeness or ridicule.

Natalie was twenty-two and she had previously worked in bars, hotels and restaurants as a waitress and she had experience of cleaning and doing general work within the hospitality sector. When the pandemic came, she had been furloughed and subsequently made redundant by a hotel in Falmouth.

'It's driving me mad, being with my mum all the time,' admitted Natalie. 'We only have one bedroom, so I have to sleep in the lounge. I've always had jobs where I can live-in before.'

Morwenna liked Natalie. She had a fresh, uninhibited manner and a ready smile. Most importantly she exuded enthusiasm and vitality. The only thing she lacked was experience as a cook. Morwenna offered her the job on the spot and hoped she wouldn't regret her hastiness. Ada was only staying for a short while, so Morwenna hoped her new employee was a quick learner. Harriet loved cooking and, all being well, she would stay until the end of the summer.

'Would you like to live-in?' asked Morwenna. 'It's not exciting here but at least you'll have your own room. Ada Bray is leaving, so if you do well you could be housekeeper by September.'

'Brilliant, when do I start?' asked Natalie without hesitation.

'Tomorrow?' suggested Morwenna, anxious to overlap Natalie's tenure with Ada's for as long as possible.

'I'll be here at nine,' replied Natalie brightly, as she bounded out of the back door.

Morwenna followed her into the kitchen garden and asked her about Catherine's death. Natalie said she had heard about the girl who died after falling off the cliff but only in the context of a local legend. She promised to check with her family to see if they knew anything. Natalie skipped down the drive and Morwenna went to look for Harriet. After searching most of the house, she located her on the top floor.

'What was Natalie like?' asked Harriet.

'She's either a gem or I've just been conned,' replied Morwenna brightly. 'I've taken her on.'

Harriet explained that she had exhausted her search of the study and she was ploughing through each room in the old servants' quarters. She was looking for the War diaries or any other paper-work of interest. There were lots of old chests and boxes and Harriet became distracted trying on ancient Edwardian and Victorian dresses and hats.

'It's a pity all the dresses are so tiny,' said Harriet, who had squeezed herself into a long, green silk dress.

She had placed the bustle underneath at the back and the gown was unfastened to allow her to breathe. She strutted up and down the landing for theatrical effect.

'Don't you look fine in that! Although I would say it is rather, erm close-fitting,' giggled Morwenna. 'We could have a fantastic fancy-dress party here.'

'Let's make it a murder-mystery,' said Harriet without thinking and then quickly corrected herself. 'Maybe not, under the circumstances.'

'We have a more pressing problem, than our murder investigation,' explained Morwenna. 'We need to clear a room for Natalie. She's starting tomorrow and she's going to be staying here!'

'Well, that's good news,' said Harriet. 'I think the room next door has the least clutter in it. Shall we clear that one?'

'No,' said Morwenna thoughtfully with her head on one side. 'I don't like the idea of staff living in servants' quarters and there are no radiators up here. Edith's is the biggest bedroom. I think we could make a small studio flat in there. Maybe fit a bathroom and kitchenette in the long run. From what you said today Ada experienced a lot of resentment towards the family and we don't want another murder in this house!'

'Also, it will be less work for us, because we've emptied most of Edith's room already,' said Harriet pragmatically.

The two women continued to search the top floor for another hour but they found no clues up there. There was an abundance of old furniture, clothing and ancient electrical equipment which was very interesting but unhelpful in terms of the murder investigation. By half-past five they were hot and covered in dust. They decided to give up hunting for the diaries for the time being, and get ready for dinner. The two women agreed to dress up, as it was their first social outing after lockdown. They chose to wear flat shoes though, because they intended to walk into Porthleven.

Ada was in the kitchen when they arrived downstairs and they tried to persuade her to come with them. She declined, offering to stay behind with Titan. Morwenna told the housekeeper that she had engaged Natalie and Ada assured her that she had heard Natalie was a good worker and, *a bit of a comedian.*

'We won't stay out late,' promised Morwenna. 'We'll need to be up early to prepare Edith's room ready for Natalie.'

Ada was surprised about Morwenna's plan to convert Edith's room into a studio-flat.

'Well times certainly are changing!' exclaimed Ada smiling and nodding with approval. 'It's a credit to you to try and do things differently. I'm not saying Miss Nancarrow did things wrong in the past but, I for one, want a different sort of world in the future.'

Morwenna was pleased with Ada's response to her decision and she privately wondered how different Ada's life might have been had she had the benefit of an education and modern opportunities. Her mind moved onto the preparations for welcoming Natalie to Gwedr Iowarth the next day.

'Harri, I've just had a thought. We need a new mattress. Natalie can't sleep in Edith's bed!' said Morwenna looking alarmed.

'Why not?' asked Harriet, naively. 'I've stripped it and the mattress is perfectly clean. We just need to find fresh sheets in the morning.' Harriet had no inhibitions about death or dead bodies.

'Edith *died* in it,' said Morwenna, stressing the word died. 'What are we going to do?'

'Don't worry,' replied Harriet. If you're that concerned, I'll order one from the internet. It'll be here tomorrow. What size is the bed?'

Morwenna and Harriet charged upstairs. The two companions were in a hurry now, because of their plans to go out for dinner. They measured the bed, which turned out to be king-size. Harriet opened her online shopping platform and typed in the choice of mattress and put it in her basket. The site asked her if she wanted a duvet, pillows and bedding so she ordered those too. Harriet liked interior design and she glanced around the room to view the current colour scheme. Based on the red and gold palette, she made a hurried decision on the duvet cover and pillow-cases and completed the order.

'OK we keep the red and gold theme. Right let's go,' said Harriet and they set off into Porthleven in haste.

Titan whined and barked when he realised the two women were leaving without him, so Ada gave him his dinner, while they slipped out of the front door. The views over the sea were fantastic even though the water was calm and it was a still, balmy evening.

Morwenna couldn't help thinking what a perfect holiday they would be having if they didn't have Catherine's murder hanging over them and her nagging suspicions about Jonathan. It was easy to minimise her fears during busy daytime activities, but when Morwenna awoke at night she ruminated. Inevitably, when her room was in shadows and she was alone, her fears became increasingly sinister. She pictured Jonathan pushing Catherine over the cliff, in her mind's eye. Then she deliberated about how she had met Jonathan, which had appeared as a chance stroke of good fortune at the time. Jonathan had been working at Bradders Bank in London when he retired. Soon after his wife had passed away, he returned to his roots in Bath and met Morwenna at a charitable function, raising money for fostering and adoption. She started to wonder whether he had traced her, perhaps using a private investigator, like Edith, and then inveigled himself into her social circle.

'Let's not talk about the murder tonight, Harri,' begged Morwenna as they walked. 'Let's pretend it's a perfectly normal evening and talk about everyday things.'

'Good idea. I guess we can't talk about time-travel in public anyway,' pointed out Harriet. 'People would think we were completely bonkers.'

Once they arrived at the restaurant, they were assigned seats outside by the harbour and the waiter advised that they should order their food and drink via the *app*. Neither Harriet nor Morwenna had ever used a restaurant app before and it took them a while to download it and successfully order what they wanted.

'It's like the world has completely changed since the pandemic,' said Morwenna shaking her head. 'You order food on mobile phone apps and bedding on computers!'

'Do you think there will be a second wave of COVID?' asked Harriet. 'Maybe over the winter.'

'I really hope not,' said Morwenna earnestly. 'I don't think I could go through this again. Do you think a vaccine is a long way off?'

'Oxford University is working with a drug company and their jab is the furthest along. But vaccine development, that can take years,' explained Harriet.

The food arrived and it looked superb. Morwenna had spicy chicken and Harriet a seafood platter. They managed to chatter through most of the meal without mentioning murder or time-travel and it felt great to return to a bit of normality. The bright half-moon rose, circled by a halo of silver light, making a silhouette of the yachts and their masts in the harbour. On the wharf, stood a procession of noble stone buildings, from bygone times with long disused out-booms.

Morwenna pictured vessels moored in the days of sailing ships and the clamour of sounds and smells on the jetty. She fancied hearing the calls of mariners as they heaved on the lines to pull ships into dock. Harriet didn't interrupt her reverie. After a while, she noticed Morwenna had returned to the real world as her faraway look had disappeared. Harriet was thankful for her companion's spiritual nature and ability to day-dream. At the moment Morwenna needed some respite from her troubles.

'I hope things work out well with Natalie,' said Harriet. 'The house is going to be a huge amount of work in the long run.'

'Especially if I'm on my own, without Jonathan,' said Morwenna. 'Edith managed things alone but I'd love to have Jonathan by my side.'

'Try to think positively for now, Wenna. Trust your instincts. You chose Jonathan and he has never done anything to let you down in the last ten years,' implored Harriet.

'Within a few days I'll have my answer, either way,' said Morwenna with a solemn face.

They ordered puddings and lingered over coffee. Morwenna was reluctant to relinquish the temporary respite from her worries. The proprietor drew on his pipe watchfully, at the entrance of the restaurant. Their table became the last to be occupied and grudgingly the two women admitted that the evening was over and they set off back to Gwedr Iowarth. Walking was hard work having eaten so much. It was fully dark when they arrived at the house.

Spectacular glittering stars crowded the pitch sky above the towering walls of Gwedr Iowarth. The two tired companions trudged up the drive and Morwenna paused on the south terrace to choose a hiding place, if she had to go back to 1962. The large oak tree looked perfectly positioned for this purpose. From there, she had a good view of the south terrace, the front of the house and she could rotate to see the drive. Looking towards the ground floor of the house she could see the front door and study window and looking upwards she could observe the windows of the two bedrooms overlooking the south terrace and the cliff edge. The oak tree was also surrounded by shrubs and the hiding place was not illuminated by the lights in the drive due to overhanging branches.

'A perfect spot. I wish I could come with you,' said Harriet longingly.

'Well, you could try,' replied Morwenna. 'Titan was able to do it, so maybe you could if we were together.'

Harriet glanced at her watch and said, 'Gosh look at the time. We'd better go to bed. I'll put my alarm on for six, we need to clean and prepare the bedroom before Natalie arrives!'

Chapter 19

The Mattress

Harriet knocked on Morwenna's door at six o'clock the next morning. Thankfully her black eye was starting to fade, so her appearance was much less alarming. Morwenna hated early mornings but she climbed out of bed straight away and they stumbled downstairs to grab a coffee and toast before getting to work in Edith's room. They even beat Ada down to breakfast which was a first.

Edith's bedroom was largely empty, so they set to work giving it a thorough vacuum, clean and polish. The room was really dusty and Harriet had to haul the vacuum cleaner downstairs several times to empty it. Leaving Morwenna busily at work, Harriet took a third trip downstairs and saw a delivery van draw up outside the house. The driver deposited the wrapped mattress, and packages containing the duvet, pillows and covers on the drive. The driver took a photo, as proof of delivery, which Harriet had never seen before. He apologised for not helping her to carry the items inside due to the COVID regulations. Harriet managed to lug the duvet and bedding upstairs on her own and she dumped them on the bedroom floor.

'You'll need to help me with the mattress, Wenna,' said Harriet who was out of breath and clammy with sweat.

'It's amazing that the stuff we ordered has arrived already,' proclaimed Morwenna. 'Let's remove the old mattress first and take it into the garden for Joseph to burn.'

Edith's mattress was extremely heavy, full of springs and very difficult to carry. It wobbled ominously as they carried it along the landing. In the end, they lost their grip and the mattress slipped down the stairs on its own and Titan had to leap out of the way to avoid a collision.

'Sorry Titan,' shouted Harriet.

Titan took the incident as an invitation to play and he started leaping on and off the mattress in the hall. He was barking and bouncing madly. He performed mock-bows to Morwenna and then, in desperation, to Harriet in an effort to entice them to join him. Eventually the two women managed distract the dog and heave the mattress away. Maybe once Natalie arrived, the three of them would be able to carry it into the part of the garden where Joseph usually lit his bonfires. The new mattress was ungainly but much lighter and easier to transport, especially as it had handles. Once they lifted the new mattress into Edith's bedroom, they both needed to sit on the floor for a few minutes to get their breath back. Harriet turned her head towards the base of Edith's four-poster bed and she spotted seven leather-bound books lined up along the central wooden slat.

'Look there are some books here, kept hidden under the mattress,' gasped Harriet excitedly.

'Let's have a look,' replied Morwenna, intrigued to find something secret.

'Harriet read aloud, '1939, 1940, 1941, 1942, 1943, 1944 and 1945. The missing diaries.'

Both women were impatient to read about the War years, but they managed to curtail their curiosity and finish preparing the room. Morwenna was pleased with the end result and admired Harriet's hasty choice of duvet covers, in a deep red with a gold trim, which matched the old room well. Ada arrived with a large jug of lemonade and two glasses. She praised their work and suggested they take a break until Natalie got there. Harriet scooped up the diaries and showed them to Ada, inquisitive to see her reaction.

'Where did you find them?' asked Ada innocently.

'Under the mattress,' replied Harriet, pointing to the bed.

'Well, that explains why she never let me turn her mattress,' said Ada. 'The crafty old devil. I hope you find what you need in them!'

'They must contain a few secrets, otherwise she wouldn't have hidden them,' concluded Morwenna.

Morwenna placed the diaries on the library table so that they could examine them later. After a few minutes and before her allotted time, Natalie arrived. She was red in the face, having dragged a very large suitcase on wheels up from the village. Her mother's house was on the far side of the harbour. Titan was the first to encounter her at the back door and he greeted her warmly, in his own way, by licking her neck which was on the level of his tongue. Ada and Harriet introduced themselves properly and Morwenna insisted that they should all be on first name terms. She also decided to draw a line in the sand about future relationships.

'We are living in the twenty-first century and I think we should be on first name terms, take it in turns to cook and eat together,' announced Morwenna. 'We'll start tonight.'

Harriet thought this was a bit rich coming from Morwenna who hated to cook, although she did more than her share of everything else.

Harriet offered to cook dinner and Ada reluctantly agreed that they should dine together that evening. Morwenna drove Natalie home to collect the rest of her possessions, which only took a few minutes. Everyone helped the newcomer carry her belongings up to Edith's room, which was officially re-named *Natalie's room*. The newcomer had very few clothes, for a young woman, but she had a large collection of sport's equipment including a surf board, tennis racquets and a hockey stick.

'I'm sports mad,' Natalie admitted to Morwenna and Harriet as they sat on the new bed, recovering from the exertions of the morning.

Ada cooked brunch and they wolfed down the sausages, bacon and egg. Titan was delighted with himself because Ada dropped one of the sausages, as she was carrying the frying pan to the kitchen table. Titan caught the sausage in his mouth before it hit the ground! After brunch, Harriet and Natalie checked that Edith's mattress contained no further secrets and they heaved it to the area Joseph reserved for bonfires.

'Surely you're not going to burn it,' proclaimed the gardener. 'It's far better than mine.'

Joseph decided to have Edith's mattress for himself, so they carried it to his cottage and removed his own for burning. Harriet and Natalie were appalled to discover that Joseph's mattress was absolutely ancient and appeared to be stuffed with straw. Once they moved the straw mattress to the bonfire area, Joseph set it alight and they stood back to watch. Flames leapt into the air and it was gone within a few seconds.

'I'm really interested in learning about gardening, Joseph,' said Natalie, through the smoke. 'Could you help me get started?'

'Yes, definitely,' replied Joseph looking shy but content. 'It would be a pleasure.'

Harriet suggested Joseph give Natalie a tour of the garden while she returned indoors to find Morwenna, whom she felt sure would be keen to start reading the diaries. Harriet found Morwenna with Ada in the kitchen and Harriet explained that she had left Natalie having an excursion around the grounds.

'I think we'll find Natalie may be happier in the garden than the house!' observed Harriet.

Morwenna made herself and Harriet a cup of coffee and they retired to the library to study the diaries. Harriet's attention became quickly devoted to reading and her friend was reluctant to interrupt her for a while. Morwenna checked Ada was out of earshot by glancing through the door into the hallway and closing it behind her.

'You were right about Ada, she's asked to leave as soon as possible,' whispered Morwenna when Harriet looked up from her reading. 'Now that probate has come through. She has her income and her house is ready.'

'Blimey what are we going to do?' asked Harriet.

'Ada says she will stay for another few days, to show Natalie the ropes and then she's off!' replied Morwenna. 'She's happy for us to contact her anytime if we need her advice.'

The two companions elected to focus on the 1943 diary. Unlike the others it was locked, and they didn't have a key, so Harriet had to break the clasp with Edith's paper knife. Morwenna was very adept at deciphering Edith's handwriting and she read the relevant sections aloud to her friend, who continued to speed-read the other diaries. Harriet had an aptitude for extracting the most important information from large documents. A skill she had developed during her medical career.

'Fifteenth of July 1943,' announced Morwenna glancing up at Harriet. *'Fred Watson has kindly provided me with a medical certificate to exempt me from Lan Army duties. He has cited, endometriosis requiring surgery, as the diagnosis. I've packed my bags and said goodbye to my friends in Lancashire. I leave for the house in Truro tomorrow…* What's endometriosis Harri?'

'It's a condition where tissue, which normally lines the womb, starts growing outside the uterus,' replied Harriet.

'Eighteenth July 1943,' continued Morwenna, after listening to Harriet's explanation. *I've settled into 42 Carclaws Street, which will be my home for the next year. Fred has promised not to tell my parents where I am. I will write to them regularly but I've had to lie and tell them I've been posted to Aberdeen with the Land Army. Fred has arranged for my food to be delivered to the house, as our family is quite well known in Truro, and I don't want to be seen. Fortunately, Daddy is really busy with the home-guard and Mummy has evacuees, so they won't have time to come looking for me. A good friend, who has been posted to Aberdeen, has agreed for me to send letters to her and she will divert them to my parents so they will have a Scottish post-mark.'*

'Oh, my goodness, they must have been having a secret relationship,' said Harriet.

'I don't think so Harri,' said Morwenna. 'I think Edith was pregnant with Catherine and Dr Watson was helping her hide the situation from her parents and from the world!'

'He can't be the father, of course,' said Harriet.

Morwenna read exerts from the diary, written intermittently over the next six months. Edith described her advancing pregnancy and her deliberations about what to do when the baby was born. Fred Watson was engaged as a doctor for local children's homes in Cornwall and from contacts in Truro, he identified the home in Helston. They selected this one so that Edith would have easy access from Porthleven after the War. Dr Watson made a donation to Helston Children's home and volunteered to become a trustee. This would lay the path for Edith to become a trustee and governor later on. It was necessary for them to have authority within the home, to ensure Edith's baby could be monitored and to make certain the child wouldn't be moved to another district. On 24th December 1943 Dr Fred Watson delivered the baby girl in the early evening and transported her to Helston Children's Home during the blackout. Edith described the pain of losing her daughter which was difficult for Morwenna to read and troubling for Harriet to listen to.

During the January of 1944, after parting with Catherine, Edith recorded much soul-searching. She condemned herself for favouring her reputation and inheritance over being with her child. The contents of the diary suggested that, had she chosen to keep her baby, she would have been disinherited by her father Jory Nancarrow. He upheld the strongest Victorian values. The later diaries confirmed that Edith regretted her decision, almost from the start. However, within six months she was a trustee at the home and then a governor within a year. The majority of Edith's earnings, as a secretary during the War, were anonymously donated to the children's home. Edith also persuaded her father to become a benefactor. Consequently, the living conditions for Catherine were far superior to the average children's home in the 1940s. Staff who did not treat the children well were quickly dismissed and those who were allowed to remain were paid above the normal wage.

'What a terrible choice for Edith,' reflected Morwenna.

'Once Catherine came to Gwedr Iowarth, Edith must have thought she possessed everything she wanted. The house, her daughter and her reputation intact. But then Catherine died and she lost the most important thing in her life. The guilt and regret must have been horrendous,' concluded Harriet.

'Does this take us forward with the identity of murderer?' enquired Morwenna.

'Not really, because only Edith and Dr Watson knew Catherine was Edith's daughter,' said Harriet.

'Could one of the family members have found out? I can't see Edith telling anyone, and Dr Watson had kept the secret for years,' said Morwenna.

'Is it possible Edith told Catherine the truth and Catherine told someone else?' asked Harriet. 'Catherine was young. She wouldn't have understood the danger she was in. The answer is in the *timing of the murder*. We have our suspects and we know who had opportunity. Something happened between Christmas Eve and New Year's Eve, that meant Catherine *had* to be killed. Catherine had been living at Gwedr Iowarth for many years. Something changed and we need to find out what that was.'

Chapter 20

Natalie and Some More Questions

Morwenna, Harriet, Ada and Natalie sat down together for dinner that evening. It was fun to have a younger person with them and Natalie's exuberance lightened the atmosphere. At first, Ada squirmed uncomfortably in her chair. After so many years of servitude, it was hard for her to relinquish the feeling that she should be waiting on others. As the meal progressed, she relaxed and fell under the spell of Natalie's easy charm.

Natalie wasn't restrained by outdated class divisions. She asked openly about events and emotions which had previously been avoided. Ada became more at ease and allowed herself to experience a feeling of acceptance, as an equal. After all, within a few days she would be in her own home and she could do as she pleased. The housekeeper looked around the room with the perspective of an independent woman. It was a good feeling. She had never sat in the dining room as a guest before, and yet every object was as familiar as her own possessions.

Morwenna saw a spark of the person Ada would have been had she not had such a difficult beginning in life and become trapped in a restrictive role. This was going to be a new era for Gwedr Iowarth and Morwenna would enjoy Ada visiting in the future.

'Morwenna,' said Natalie. 'I'm keen to learn about gardening, could I work with Joseph Penhaligon for a day each week?'

'Yes fine,' she replied, 'Joseph could do with some help.'

'I'm happy to do most of the cooking and shopping for now,' said Harriet, accepting that Morwenna much preferred cleaning to cooking.

'Well, that leaves me to relax in the sitting room and be waited on hand and foot. I wonder if we can have those call-bells working?' laughed Morwenna.

'Don't think you're ringing for me, m'lady,' said Harriet to her friend. 'This isn't *Upstairs Downstairs*.'

'What's *Upstairs Downstairs*?' asked Natalie curiously.

'It was a TV programme in the 1970s. Something like *Downton Abbey*,' explained Ada. 'The call-bells still work. There is one by each fireplace.'

Morwenna looked towards the fireplace and she noticed a gold cord with a tassel on the end hanging to the side of the fire surround.

'I'm only joking of course,' she clarified. 'I'll help with the cleaning and carry on with the sorting and de-cluttering. Ada, you need to teach Natalie and I, all the information we need to run the house. For example, how to turn the water off and all those little secrets about how things work and where things are kept.'

Ada was relieved that she was able to retire before August. She had received her first pension payment from the trust-fund the previous day and that, combined with her state pension, would be adequate to give her a secure lifestyle in Falmouth. Ada admitted that looking after Miss Nancarrow and running the house had become far too much for her over the past few years. She was looking forward to returning to amateur dramatics and spending time reading, which was her great passion.

Ada opened up that evening and they saw a more relaxed side to her personality. She was well informed, interesting and sensitive to those around her, making her very good company. It occurred to Morwenna that Ada was the last of a repressed generation of servants who had been required to supress their spirit and aspirations in the service of others.

Harriet wondered about Ada's participation in amateur dramatics. She was more mistrustful than Morwenna and the possibility that the housekeeper was acting in a more open and relaxed manner could be a subterfuge to conceal her guilt. Harriet chose to keep her suspicions quiet for the time being.

'I've ordered a *man and a van* to collect my things,' Ada informed the group. 'Then I can just take one or two suitcases with the last of my clothes when I finish next week.'

'I'll be sorry to see you go. You'll have to come back and see us regularly,' said Morwenna. 'Have a browse around the house tonight and choose some furniture, pictures and ornaments to take with you. This place is far too cluttered and it'll be less for Natalie and me to clean! I need to make space for some of my things from Bath when I move in permanently.'

'That's assuming you don't discover I'm a murderer and have me put in prison!' said Ada, as if she had been reading Harriet's thoughts.

Natalie looked seriously alarmed at this moment, because they hadn't told her the details of the investigation and Harriet's blackboard of suspects. Harriet asked Morwenna if it was OK, and then offered Natalie a potted history of the evidence they had collected in relation to Catherine's death and their recent efforts to find the culprit. Natalie said she wasn't totally surprised because her grandmother had been the cook at Gwedr Iowarth at the time of Catherine's death and she had spoken about the tragedy.

'Is your grandmother still alive, Natalie?' asked Harriet.

'Gosh no, she died when I was about twelve and she was pretty old then.'

'What were her views on Catherine's death?' enquired Morwenna.

'Nan told mum that she was subjected to a very severe grilling by the police, even though she wasn't present in the house at the time Catherine died,' described Natalie. 'It was quite frightening because, in those days, servants could be accused of crimes to protect more *important* people. They required her husband to sign a statement to swear she came home by nine thirty and she didn't return to Gwedr Iowarth until the following day.'

'What else did she say?' persisted Harriet, who was very keen to gather every detail she could.

'She told me about Joseph Penhaligon and his illness,' whispered Natalie. 'Lots of the people from the village pointed at him. There was a lot of prejudice about mental health problems in those days.'

'Did your grandmother think Joseph was involved?' continued Harriet.

'No absolutely not. She said he was a very gentle person but they still locked him up in an asylum for a while,' replied Natalie. 'That's why she was frightened. The servants thought they could be blamed.'

Did your grandmother say anything else?' asked Morwenna.

'She informed the police about the missing pepper-pot. It was an odd thing, but when my grandmother left the house on New Year's Eve, the salt and pepper pots were on the kitchen table. The next day the pepper-pot was gone and it couldn't be found. The police searched the house and grounds, not specifically for that, but it was never recovered,' explained Natalie.

'Well, you can't kill someone with pepper, can you?' said Morwenna lightly.

'It was odd though,' interjected Ada. 'I'd forgotten about the pepper-pot. We still have the salt-pot and I had to buy a new pepper-pot because the old one was never located. The original salt and pepper pots were *Masons Regency*. The pattern with the blue and yellow flowers and the oriental bird. I like the design. You'll see quite a lot of it, in the kitchen cupboards. I could never find a matching one though, so the replacement was a plain white one.'

Harriet privately wondered if pepper could have been used to disable the victim, but she didn't express her suspicions. She considered the possibility of pepper being thrown in Catherine's face to enable a weaker assailant to gain the upper-hand. In Harriet's view, this could point to a female attacker, as a male could rely on his physical strength to push his victim over the railings. She also noted that Ada had never provided this information when she had interviewed her. Ada could have forgotten about the missing pepper-pot over time *or* she was trying to protect a female assailant such as herself.

'Do you mind if I make a project of the tennis court?' asked Natalie, changing the subject.

'You mean making preparations for it to be played on?' asked Morwenna, looking up from her food in surprise.

'Yes. I love tennis,' said Natalie, 'and it would be something I can get my teeth into.'

'Blimey, it sounds very ambitious to me,' said Harriet. 'But it would be brilliant to have the grass tennis court back in use. Morwenna and I love tennis. I wonder when it was last played on?'

'Not since the summer of 1962,' clarified Ada. 'At first Joseph kept it mown and rolled but then Miss Nancarrow told Joseph to let it go, because it wouldn't be used and it was a lot of work to keep the lawn in playable condition. Catherine loved sport, especially tennis. Miss Nancarrow arranged for her to have professional tennis lessons and she became very proficient. Joseph occasionally runs the lawnmower over the court, to keep the weeds down, but I think it would take a lot of work to be able to use it again.'

'We might have to have it re-turfed,' said Natalie passionately. 'I used to help with the grass courts when I worked at the Imperial Victoria Hotel in Torquay. I'll have a look in the sheds and summerhouse to see what tools we already have and draw up a budget for the specialist turf. You have to use perennial ryegrass.'

Harriet and Morwenna were inspired by Natalie's enthusiasm which was contagious and raised everybody's spirits. They believed Natalie was going to be a great asset. She had been excited with her bedroom allocation, stating that it was the largest bedroom she had ever seen. Natalie was very pleased with the idea of having a plumber to fit an en suite bathroom, so she could have a partially self-contained living space. She was very thankful to Ada for putting her name forward for the position. Natalie's mother was glad to have her out of the house but she had been troubled about Catherine's death which she considered very sinister. Although Natalie reminded her mother, that after Ada retired, there would be no one left who had been at Gwedr Iowarth in 1962 except for Joseph in the cottage.

Natalie and Ada offered to clear away and Harriet and Morwenna retreated to the study and lit the fire. The evening was unseasonably cold.

'I wonder what happened to Catherine's father?' mused Morwenna, as she warmed her feet in front of the fire.

'I guess the obvious hypothesis would be that he was an American GI, she met while in the Land Army. There was nothing about him in the war diaries, nor anything in the diaries we found in the safe,' said Harriet.

They retrieved the Land Army photographs from the library and noted Edith had been stationed in Halton near Lancaster. A brief search on the internet revealed that many American GIs had been processed through the army camp in Halton but they had no clues to take this line of enquiry further forward.

'I suppose if Catherine's body was exhumed, her DNA might lead us to family members in America, if that's where her father was from. It would be a bit far-fetched to think her father might have returned to kill her, especially since he may not have even known she existed in the first place,' said Harriet.

'If Edith had traced Catherine's father, she wouldn't have left it for twenty years and then contacted him, would she?' mused Morwenna.

Harriet thought it was best to keep an open mind, so she added, *Catherine's father,* to the suspect list even though they didn't have a name for him.

'It's possible her father became important or well-known and came back to kill Catherine to protect his identity and reputation,' postulated Harriet, without any real conviction in her voice.

Ada popped her head around the door, to wish them goodnight. Morwenna beckoned her to join them and she took the window-seat.

Morwenna tapped the diaries and went straight to the point, 'Edith was Catherine's mother.'

Ada's mouth dropped open and, unless she was a *very* good actress, it appeared that Ada had no idea.

'It must have crossed your mind,' proposed Harriet, while scrutinising the expression on Ada's face.

'It did occur to me, but Miss Nancarrow never appeared interested in men,' said Ada cautiously. 'She was a confirmed spinster. It certainly explains the amount of money she gave to the children's home and the amount of time she spent helping there. As a child, I remember that whenever we were short staffed or needed someone to help with taking the children on holiday, Miss Nancarrow would be there. It must have cost her a fortune. The children were given new beds, new clothes, a playroom. When central heating was fitted the kids thought they were in seventh heaven!'

'I guess she had to give things to benefit all the children to ensure Catherine received what she needed, without giving herself away,' concluded Morwenna.

'From what I've heard about Edith's father, he would have been furious, if he'd have known,' mused Harriet.

'Would Jory Nancarrow have disowned Edith if he had been aware of her pregnancy?' Morwenna asked Ada.

'From what I've gathered about him from Miss Nancarrow, the answer to that question, would have been *yes*,' said Ada. 'He was very upright and a highly religious man and there were no second chances. Remember he never let Frank Nancarrow back into his business and he kept him out of his will permanently after he gambled some of the family's money.'

'What would have been Frank's reaction to Edith having a child?' asked Harriet.

'Oh my God,' gasped Ada. 'Did he know about Catherine?'

'We're pretty sure he didn't, but what if he had been made aware of the situation?' asked Harriet.

'He would have been very upset. He was bitter about his lack of finances but if he had known about Catherine, things would have been far worse,' said Ada.

'Angry enough to kill?' enquired Harriet.

'I never saw him become violent. A weak man, I would say, not a killer. A whinger certainly. I honestly can't see him killing Catherine though. He was more of a manipulator. Perhaps he might have tried to blackmail Miss Nancarrow?' suggested Ada.

'Are you off to bed Ada?' asked Morwenna, thinking Harriet had interrogated Ada enough.

'Yes, did you mean it about taking some things for my new house?' asked Ada producing a list from her pocket. 'Have a look through this and tell me if your happy with my requests?'

Morwenna looked down the list which appeared very modest including the armchairs and table from Ada's sitting room, her own bed and bedroom furniture. Ada had also chosen a few pretty water-colours from the morning room, some china ornaments and a small carriage clock.

'I can't take anything big,' Ada explained, 'and I've bought all new white goods and kitchen equipment already. I've made the curtains and the carpets went down today. I'm keen to take the armchairs because I covered them myself.'

'That's absolutely fine,' said Morwenna. 'That will leave some space in the morning room for my pictures from Bath.'

'My last night here, will be Monday,' said Ada. 'If that's OK with you?'

'That's fine,' confirmed Morwenna, 'One of us will drive you over to Falmouth first thing on Tuesday morning with the last of your things.'

After Ada retired to bed, Harriet and Morwenna decided to plan a small leaving party for Ada on Monday. It would have to take place outdoors because of the COVID pandemic. They would invite Joseph Penhaligon, Emily Watson and ask Natalie to invite some of Ada's friends from the village such as Natalie's mother. She had earned a good send-off, after all her years of service.

'Sunday is D-day,' Morwenna reminded Harriet. 'If we've not iden-tified the murderer by then, I'm going back to 1962.'

'I understand,' nodded Harriet wearing a sombre expression. 'Maybe something will crop up before then?'

Harriet retired to bed and Morwenna decided to revisit the library to select some books for Ada to take to Falmouth. She thought there may be some classic novels or early editions that she could give Ada as a leaving present. She scoured the shelves and picked out some fine leather-bound copies of the Jane Austen and early editions of other classic authors which she put to one side.

Morwenna was very interested in old books and so she became distracted looking at the different titles on the shelves. The novels repre-sented the tastes of the Nancarrow's from 1880 to the present day. There were many religious texts inscribed with the name, Jory Nancarrow, in archaic copper-plate script. Her eyes fell on a book called, *The Land Girls of World War II* by Audrey F Tristan. Morwenna opened it, to see Edith's name written inside the front cover. To her surprise she discovered a letter with the name, *Morwenna,* penned in Edith's familiar handwriting. She fell on the envelope and prised it open with her thumb. A single flimsy sheet floated onto the library table and Morwenna examined it eagerly.

25th June 1987

Dear Morwenna,

Well done, if you've come this far. I really needed to trust you before you found out my precious secret about Catherine. By now you know she was my daughter. All the secrecy seems ridiculous nowadays and, no doubt by the time I die (I don't intend to die very soon), it will be quite common place for a white woman to have a bi-racial child. But in those days, you had to be incredibly courageous to keep a baby in the situation I found myself. And I'm afraid I wasn't that brave. Dr Fred Watson had been widowed and had Catherine's father been white, Fred would have married me and no one would have found out. My father would have thrown me into the street, had he discovered my pregnancy and that is no exaggeration. However, this is not an excuse. I made the wrong decision and I should have kept Catherine and sacrificed Gwedr Iowarth. My mistake led to the tragedy of losing Catherine and I had a very long time to repent.

You may ask why I didn't 'come clean' when my father died. After all, by then, I was the mistress of my own destiny. But there were several reasons to keep the secret. Firstly, Fred Watson had helped me by taking Catherine to the children's home. We could still have been prosecuted for abandoning a baby and he may have been struck-off the medical register. Secondly, I knew that my family would be very bitter towards Catherine and may treat her badly, although I never thought anyone would kill her. Lastly, I was a coward. I wanted to keep my so-called reputation, the house and the money. I never told Catherine

*about her identity because she was young and she would have
been tempted to tell others. The only other person in my confi-
dence was Fred Watson, and he was beyond suspicion. He feared
our secret getting out more than me because he had to work to
support Emily. Of course, as you've realised, this still doesn't tell
us who killed Catherine so I'm hoping you can use more modern
methods to find out what really happened.*

This is my last letter, so you don't need to look for anymore!
Good luck
Love Edith

Well thanks very much Edith, Morwenna thought to herself. It looks
like I'm going back to 1962 and I just hope I return from there alive!
She looked up and saw a sizeable collection of modern science fiction,
time travel literature and magical fiction. That's funny, she thought, I
wasn't expecting Edith to read that sort of thing. However, the volumes
had been well-thumbed, so she presumed either Ada or Edith must have
been the reader. Morwenna enjoyed books about time travel herself, so
she knew about the dangerous outcomes of going back in time, if one
was to inadvertently change something. Her eyes progressed from the
time travel section to magic and wizardry.

'Well, at least I'm not a wizard!' said Morwenna aloud, thinking
everyone was in bed.

'Thank God for that!' said Natalie, who had just arrived at the library
door. 'I'm off to bed. I've planned out the tennis court and estimated
costs for the new turf. I promise to do some cleaning tomorrow unless
you have a magical spell we could use instead?'

They hadn't told Natalie or anyone else about visiting the past, so
Morwenna conceded that Natalie must regard some of her behaviours
as markedly strange. Morwenna wondered if she would ever share her
experiences of time-travel because she feared no one could accept it.
She scarcely believed it herself. She climbed the stairs and patted Titan's
rough head as she left him on his rug.

She pushed the letter under Harriet's door, so she could read it first thing in the morning. Before retiring to bed, Morwenna briefly gazed out of her bedroom window. It was after midnight and the heavens were obliterated by mist. A lighthouse blinked faintly, and she wondered what Jonathan was doing right now and whether he could see the stars. The pain of missing him was visceral. Soon she would know the identity of Catherine's killer, and she only hoped her marriage would survive the truth.

Chapter 21

The Wait

It was still foggy when Morwenna awoke the next morning. She was painfully aware that she only had one more night before she would have to return to 1962, if they couldn't make any headway with the investigation. She looked at her watch and noted it was eight in the morning, so she tried calling Jonathan. She continued to hear the message stating the number could not be connected. As expected, Titan was waiting for her in his usual spot. He had accepted Natalie without any protest and regarded her as a friend but he was loyal to Morwenna, his favourite human. He thumped his tail on the ground and trotted down the hall, his fur brushing her side. Titan only condescended to spending time with the other women if they were going to feed him, play with him or take him for a walk.

Ada, Natalie and Harriet were busy in the kitchen. Morwenna entered and briefly paused to observe the hustle and bustle. It was a cheerful scene, but she felt an outsider, somehow. Harriet was engrossed in combining the ingredients for bread making. Ada was schooling Natalie on the contents of the storage cupboards, ordering systems and how to work the various appliances including the washing machine and tumble drier. The housekeeper was clothed in a black dress, brown tights and flat shoes. Natalie, on the other hand, was wearing tight black jeans, men's work boots and an oversized colourful striped sweater. However, they seemed to be getting on fine so Morwenna crept passed, little noticed.

She took her coffee outdoors with Titan at her heals. She traversed the kitchen garden, hoping Natalie had plans for a vegetable patch because there was certainly wasted potential there. She aimlessly plucked some chives from the overgrown garden. She sniffed the herbs, then started to munch on them, as she strolled.

The morning air was sharp in her nostrils, as Morwenna crossed the south terrace. A cool sea mist drifted on the horizon. She took up position behind the large oak tree, which was surrounded by shrubbery. Morwenna sat down and encouraged Titan to join her in the under-growth. He seemed happy to stay close by. It was going to be very cold on Sunday night in 1962 and Morwenna decided she needed to wear several layers. From this vantage point, she was confident she would be able to cover the drive, the south facing windows, the terrace, the front door and anyone emerging from the kitchen garden when they exited the kitchen. She intended to re-visit her planned position once it was dark that evening, to ensure she would not miss anything and to check the lighting. As Morwenna was crawling out of her hiding place, Natalie came around the corner and caught her just as she emerged. Titan and his mistress were covered in soil and leaves.

'Harriet says breakfast is ready,' Natalie said smirking. She refrained from making any comment on Morwenna's peculiar behaviour.

'Just looking for Titan's ball,' said Morwenna weakly. 'Lost it yesterday!'

'Are you coming to the dining room on foot or will you fly there on your broom?' Natalie asked, grinning at her employer, and implying she hadn't forgotten Morwenna's previous comments about *not* being a wizard.

Morwenna followed Natalie through the front door and into the dining room, determined to act as normally as possible for the rest of the day. Natalie was full of questions about the house and garden. Her enthusiasm was joyous and Ada almost felt sorry she was leaving. After breakfast, Morwenna and Harriet met in the library to review their evidence. Harriet had already added Edith's pregnancy and Dr Fred Watson's involvement in the birth of Catherine. While it was lovely to have Edith's letter, they were no further forward in finding the killer.

The missing pepper-pot pointed towards a female assailant but didn't exonerate any of the other suspects.

Morwenna and Harriet reviewed the timing of each suspect's individual movements on New Year's Eve and how this would influence Morwenna's surveillance operation.

'I think you need to be in place from about midnight,' suggested Harriet. 'Catherine went to bed at twelve thirty and you need to ensure you pick up any activities on the terrace before that.'

'I agree,' said Morwenna, 'and then I'll just wait and observe what happens, although it would be tempting to intervene to stop the murder.'

Harriet viewed Morwenna sternly and reminded her of the dangers of time travel, 'If you prevent Catherine's death, you have changed the past itself. An alteration in the course of history could result in any number of possible permutations, even the possibility of *you* ceasing to exist!'

'I know, I know,' replied Morwenna. 'I'm just there to honour Edith's wishes and hopefully save my marriage.'

Morwenna noticed that Harriet had placed the *Masons* salt pot on the library table. She picked it up and studied it for a moment. It was a squat object with a pretty blue and yellow pattern. The salt pot had one hole at the top but the pepper pot would have had multiple holes. Underneath was a round opening, about a centimetre in diameter, containing a cork stopper. Harriet had replaced the contents of the salt-shaker with pepper. In order to demonstrate, she removed the cork, shook the pot and a significant handful of fine white pepper fell into her hand.

'I think Catherine's assailant somehow used this to disable her before killing her. I remember an elderly lady, a neighbour of mine, telling me that in the 1950s women carried pepper wrapped in a handkerchief. To throw in the face of any would-be attacker,' explained Harriet. 'That's why I think Catherine's killer was more likely to be a woman.'

'I've heard of that strategy before, for women to protect themselves and I suppose a man would be less likely to think of it. Golly Harriet you are clever, but even if we assume the killer was a woman that still leaves us with quite a few suspects: Ada Bray, Emily Watson, Mavis Nancarrow and my mother Ebrel,' reflected Morwenna.

'I accept that you don't want to hear this Wenna,' said Harriet cautiously and keeping a neutral expression, 'but Ebrel would be high up on my list of suspects. If she realised Catherine was Edith's daughter, she would have the most to gain by killing her. Ebrel was likely to inherit when Edith died. Ebrel wasn't to know she would be killed in an airline disaster years before her time.'

'I thought the same, but remember my second name is Catherine,' reasoned Morwenna. 'I never placed any importance on my middle name before but I think I could be named after Catherine Nicholas.'

'Hm, calling your daughter after a person you murdered would be unconventional, to say the least,' conceded Harriet. 'But we must keep an open mind.'

Harriet and Morwenna couldn't find any further lines of enquiry to pursue that day. They had studied the diaries and sorted through all the paper-work in the house. They spent a futile hour taking every book off the shelf in the library and shaking it, to check for hidden documents or letters. They didn't find anything of interest. Edith had left quite a few notes in books, but these were often shopping lists or comments on the plot or content of the book. At midday Harriet returned to the kitchen to prepare lunch and take the bread out of the oven. Morwenna joined Ada and Natalie for the *house briefing,* as Natalie called it. The housekeeper showed them the electricity, water and gas meters, the stop-tap, the fuse box and switches to control the outside lights. There were countless little quirks in the house. For example, how to stop the overflow in the bathroom running, by lifting the ballcock in the toilet. Natalie was leaving nothing to chance and she had a folder containing lined A4 sheets which were filed in alphabetical order. Every instruction was written down. She was taking her future housekeeping duties seriously.

Next Ada took them to the key hooks and cupboards behind the kitchen door. She had labelled each key. There were two back door keys, one labelled *back door key* and one *spare back door key.*

'Those keys look pretty old,' commented Morwenna. 'Are they original or have the locks been changed?'

'No, they are the same as the ones we had when I came here,' confirmed Ada, 'but the bolts are new. William Penhaligon fitted them, after Catherine died. We had to tighten up on security which had been very lax before then. Although I don't usually bother with the bolts nowadays.'

Ada pointed to the cupboards underneath the key hooks. There was a small tool kit for day-to-day jobs, a new first aid kit and an ancient one, several pots of paint for emergency touch-ups and a very large can of adhesive.

'Marvellous stuff, this wood glue,' remarked Ada, 'I discovered it a few years ago and it fixes anything!'

Natalie laboriously scribbled down all she needed and requested the phone numbers for the tradesmen Ada usually employed, if anything went wrong.

'Do we have any winter coats in the house?' asked Morwenna, once the briefing was over.

'Well, it's a bit warm at the moment,' replied Ada, 'but there are some overcoats hanging here and a couple of winter coats in the cloak room, off the hall.'

Morwenna searched the cloak room and found a very thick, black, long fur coat. It was a musty and moth-eaten. It would be warm and, importantly, the dark colour would help her merge into the shadows. *Perfect*, she thought to herself. She was becoming more excited and less fearful about her forthcoming adventure. This time she had formulated a plan, so things were less risky. She would conduct a rehearsal tonight with Harriet pretending to be Catherine. She wouldn't go through the mirror, of course. The rehearsal would remain in 2020.

Morwenna heard Harriet sound the gong, and she trotted to the dining room, hungrily. At first, she had thought the bell was a bit pretentious, but it saved people yelling at the top of their voice to attract attention. Since Harriet had been cooking, the style of the food had advanced thirty years. Today she served an anchovy salad with rocket. Ada wasn't used to this type of food and she placed her hand over her mouth, to hide her distaste. She was looking forward to returning to her own style of cooking next week in her new home. In the meantime, Ada was grateful to have some time off before she left Gwedr Iowarth.

'I've looked through your estimates of the supplies you need for the tennis court,' said Morwenna to Natalie. 'Go ahead and order what you want. The bank sent me a visa card to access a domestic current account for the house and garden, so you can order what you need online. I've put the card in the safe but you can just ask me for it when you need it.'

'That's going to be a lot easier than Miss Nancarrow's system. I used to take a signed cheque to the bank for cash and then keep a ledger. It became a real problem once the pandemic hit and Miss Nancarrow was poorly. I had to keep far too much money in the house, which made me uncomfortable,' reflected Ada. 'There's about two thousand pounds in the tin in the kitchen drawer and the cash book is in there too, if you need it.'

The gloom lifted soon after lunch and a sage watery sun broke through. Morwenna and Harriet set out for a ramble with Titan. It gave them the chance to make plans for that night's rehearsal, after the others retired to bed. Neither Ada's nor Natalie's room overlooked the south terrace so they wouldn't be watched. The sun grew quite hot and the remaining mist evaporated as they walked. On the way back, they settled down, on the beach beneath Gwedr Iowarth, to relax and soak up the warmth. After a while, Morwenna became restless and picked her way through the boulders to approach the base of the cliff. She shuddered to think of Catherine being pushed over the railings to be smashed on the rocks below. At least Morwenna wouldn't have to see her hit the rocks and she certainly didn't intend to look over the railings when she went back in time.

Harriet joined her and they commenced a hunt for the pepper-pot, turning over boulders and examining rock pools. It was fruitless, of course, had the pepper-pot been thrown over the cliff, the pieces would have been noticed at the time or they would have been swept out to sea during storms. Harriet found a couple of tiny caverns and recesses in the cliff wall, but again there was nothing inside them except seaweed and shells that had become wedged there during high tides. Morwenna shouted for Titan and they trudged back up the stone steps. Harriet searched fissures and crevices in the rocky stairs as they climbed, but she found nothing.

'Even if we found the pepper-pot, it wouldn't lead us to the killer, unless finger prints can last fifty years,' said Morwenna.

When they returned to the house Harriet researched the question about how long finger prints could last using the internet and scribbled down her findings to share with Morwenna:

Fingerprints decay over time. After a variable period, they disappear altogether. They can last for days or years. Research has shown that some fingerprints can survive for several years on a shiny surface. On a porous or rough surface, they are less enduring. Their longevity can depend on the presence of substances such as sweat or grease on the person's hands and the surrounding conditions in terms of humidity, light and temperature. They are likely to last longer inside than out. In 1956 a murder was solved thirty years after it happened, by identifying finger prints on a piece of glass because it had been stored in perfect conditions.

Morwenna joined Harriet in the kitchen and watched her assembling the necessary ingredients for supper. Harriet had noticed Ada's reluctance with the anchovy and rocket salad so she was preparing something a bit more traditional, shepherd's pie. Ada was packing tea chests in her room and carefully wrapping the watercolours she had selected from the morning room. Natalie had been helping Ada pack most of the afternoon because the van was coming for her possessions first thing the next morning which was Sunday or *D-Day* as Morwenna had described it to Harriet. Natalie returned to the kitchen and asked Harriet to explain to her, how shepherd's pie was cooked.

'I'm good at cleaning, serving drinks and I like gardening but I hardly know any cookery. I don't even know the basics,' Natalie admitted candidly. 'My mother only has a tiny flat and we mostly ate microwave meals and takeaways.'

'Because your grandmother was a professional cook, I presumed she would have passed the knowledge through the family,' said Harriet.

'She didn't unfortunately,' remarked Natalie, 'but I intend to learn. I've really enjoyed the food since I came here.'

Natalie whipped out her folder and turned to the section marked recipes and cooking. As Harriet cooked, Natalie wrote down the ingredients and method. Harriet showed her how to peel potatoes and carrots. She laboriously shaved each vegetable and chopped the onions. It took her a while but she was pleased with the results.

'I've bought a few different spirits and mixers from the supermarket to refresh the drinks cabinet,' said Harriet, 'so perhaps you can mix us some cocktails tonight? There's a great 1930's cocktail cabinet next to the gramophone in the sitting room. The booze was ancient so I threw it away, but there is a cocktail shaker and some really trendy retro cocktail glasses.'

Ada appeared in the kitchen, hearing the last part of the conversation and she reached for a book on how to prepare cocktails, from the shelf above the kitchen sink.

'There you are,' said the housekeeper, with a relaxed smile. 'That's an original cocktail recipe book. Much beloved recipes of Frank and Mavis Nancarrow. Mavis especially liked a fancy cocktail. I have fresh lemons and a jar of cherries, if that will help.'

Ada lifted another item off the shelf. This was a battered exercise book, wrapped in brown paper. The cover was ancient, torn and there were fat stains on it.

'This recipe book was given to me by your grandmother, Natalie. When she came here in the 1950's. She initially lived-in and she recorded the methods from the cook who was here before her. By the time I came here in 1962, your grandmother was married and lived in the village. Live-in servants were going out of vogue by then. Anyway, you may find it very useful, especially for baking. I'm not taking it with me. I rarely use recipes nowadays, all the knowledge is up here,' Ada said, pointing to her head.

'Brilliant, thanks,' said Natalie.

Natalie took a bottle of rosé wine out of the fridge and decanted it into ice cube trays.

'For later,' Natalie said, tapping the side if her nose.

There was a modest merriment at supper. This was incongruous with Morwenna's dark mood. The food was pleasant, if not a little bland, and the evening dragged in spite of Natalie's innovative cocktails. The general favourite was *Pineapple Sparkle* . Natalie had taken the wine ice cubes, placed them in a bag and smashed them with the rolling pin. This provided the base for the cocktail. She poured pineapple liqueur, over the iced wine. Harriet became a bit tipsy, but Morwenna only had a couple of drinks, to ensure she was coherent for the *murder rehearsal,* later on. Ada was the first to retire to bed at about half past ten and Natalie went up about eleven thirty. She explained that she had bought subscription TV and had become hooked on the box-sets and she intended to binge watch a few more episodes.

Once Natalie was safely out of the way, Morwenna retrieved the fur coat from the cloak room and they left via the front door to reach the south terrace. Morwenna and Titan concealed themselves in the bushes surrounding the oak tree and Harriet took up Catherine's position next to the railings guarding the cliff. Morwenna crouched in the bushes and Harriet spoke nonsense aloud at her normal volume. Morwenna could hear her clearly and she could see all her intended vantage points by the light of the lamp on the drive. She gave Titan a dog-treat every few minutes, out of her pocket, which succeeded in keeping him still and quiet. This rehearsal would serve as an incentive to keep him calm for the *real* event. Harriet, on the other hand, could not see Morwenna in the undergrowth because the bushes were shaded from the outside lights by the branches of the oak tree. The two women agreed that the plan could not be improved upon and they both went to bed.

Morwenna gazed out of her window, before she fell into bed, safe in the knowledge that tomorrow she would discover the identity of Catherine's killer. It's a pity Edith would never have known the truth, she thought to herself, unless she risked changing history, and that could be very dangerous.

Chapter 22

D-Day

Ada was up long before anyone else on Sunday. She completed the finishing touches to her packing except two small cases of clothes and her toiletries to take with her, when she left for good, on Tuesday. For her last two nights she would be sleeping in Catherine's old room, on the first floor, because her bedroom furniture would be in Falmouth. Natalie and Harriet were up next and they started to carry down the boxes and tea-chests from Ada's room.

The removal van was expected at half past nine. Next, they carried the packages containing the watercolours from the morning room onto the drive. Between Harriet and Natalie, who was surprisingly strong, they carried Ada's mattress, bed base and dressing table downstairs. They would have to ask the van driver to help them with the wardrobe. Finally, Harriet and Natalie removed the items Ada wanted from her sitting room, the former butler's pantry. There were two armchairs, which Ada had recently had re-covered in a floral-patterned fabric. Natalie secretly thought the material was hideous, but she said nothing. Ada was also taking a small kitchen table, four chairs, a sideboard and rug which had been in her sitting room. When Morwenna got up, she wheeled Ada's ancient black and white TV out of the house.

'You could buy a multi-media, flat-screen TV?' suggested Natalie.

'I've not heard of one of those,' said Ada looking puzzled. 'Although I have bought myself a computer and a router. I've not taken them out of their boxes yet. I rather like the way you can make video calls and order things off the internet. Perhaps you can help me set them up Natalie?'

'No problem. If its ok with Morwenna, I'll come with you today and get everything working for you,' replied Natalie.

The van arrived and the driver and Natalie managed to carry Ada's wardrobe down two-flights of stairs, without doing them any serious damage. The van set off to Ada's house and Ada, Natalie and Harriet followed by car.

Morwenna remained behind at Gwedr Iowarth but found she couldn't settle to anything. She roamed around the house vaguely searching for clues. Harriet had warned her several times that she should not attempt to change history by either preventing the murder or interacting with anyone from the past. Morwenna had the niggling feeling that she was missing something vital in relation to Edith. She considered telling her great aunt the identity of the murderer when she went back to 1963 and then realised that would have serious repercussions in terms of changing the course of history. She contemplated leaving Edith a message, to be found much later on, but couldn't think of any way of doing this reliably. In any event, this would almost certainly change her great aunt's future activities.

While in the sitting room, Morwenna had a brain-wave. *What an idiot,* she thought to herself. *The answer is staring me in the face.* She opened the secret drawer in the sideboard. She removed the key for the grandfather clock and unlocked the glass door covering the clock face. Morwenna went to the kitchen and returned with the tool box. She searched through the wrenches until she found one which would open the nuts holding the clockface in place. She kept the smallest wrench and put the rest away. Morwenna collected the large tin of glue and the spare back door key from the kitchen. She placed the adhesive, the wrench and the spare back door key in the deep pockets of the fur coat, she planned to wear on her adventure.

She prayed Harriet would forgive her. The rest of the day crawled by. Morwenna tried to read a book but took nothing in. It seemed like forever before the others returned from Falmouth. Keeping secrets from

Harriet weighed on Morwenna's conscience but she didn't want any more lectures on the dangers of dabbling with time.

On arrival at Ada's house, Harriet and Ada supervised the positioning of furniture and Natalie unpacked the new lap-top and set it up. She took the router out of its box and plugged it into the phone line. Within fifteen minutes she had achieved what would have taken Ada hours. The new homeowner was delighted with her computer and Natalie spent a while showing her how to use the internet, search for information and order things. On the way back, Ada offered to buy fish and chips, so no one had to bother with preparing lunch.

Morwenna didn't enjoy her meal, as she was starting to feel distinctly queasy. In the end, she decided to tell the others she felt unwell and she retired to bed until dinner time. She hadn't slept well the night before, so Morwenna manged to win a few hours of fitful sleep, being awoken by Harriet half an hour before dinner was ready. The dinner was lasagne which was normally one of Morwenna's favourites but she picked at her food, like a sparrow. Natalie and Ada sensed Morwenna wasn't herself and they withdrew to the kitchen to tidy-up and play cards. Harriet went through the final plans with Morwenna and reminded her that she was *an observer not a participant.*

'Of course,' said Morwenna, 'I won't do anything stupid! Don't worry if I'm gone for quite a while. I'm going to stay until all the new-year guests have left and the house guests are in bed, just so I don't miss anything.'

At eleven o'clock Morwenna departed upstairs and dressed in thick trousers and a couple of jumpers. On top of that she wore the fur coat, a hat and gloves. Harriet, Morwenna and Titan left by the back door and crossed the garden to the mirror. It was a warm evening so Morwenna was sweating. It was half past eleven by the time they reached their destination. Harriet passed her friend the torch and wished her good luck.

'Be careful, Wenna,' said Harriet. 'For God's sake, don't do anything stupid!'

Morwenna was ready for this. She held Titan by the collar and they glided easily through the mirror. Harriet tried to follow a few paces behind, but was met by a firm, cold sheet of glass. There was no way she was going through, so Harriet kicked the wall with frustration and shouted to Morwenna that she would wait close by.

As Morwenna passed through the mirror, she felt queer and confused for a moment. She paused to check her pockets for the glue, the wrench and the spare back door key. The ritual of double-checking her equipment enabled her to recover her presence of mind. Harriet was blissfully unaware of her *additional* plan. Morwenna proceeded decisively around the house anti-clockwise. She glimpsed through the French doors into the sitting room and the New Year party was in full-flow. She called Titan to heal and didn't linger for long. She continued past the study window, crossed the terrace and located the oak tree with her torch. The bushy undergrowth at the base of the tree was a little more spartan than in the rehearsal, but there was still plenty to hide in. Morwenna was thankful for her layers of clothing as she settled down on the stony ground which was ice cold and hard with frost.

Titan was not particularly perturbed and he was happy to receive a dog treat every so often. He remained still and his breath warmed Morwenna's cheek. His closeness was a comfort to his mistress. She illuminated her digital watch and it read quarter to twelve.

Phillipe Bouvier came to the front door alone and smoked a slim cigar. He was illuminated by the lights from the hall and Morwenna observed that he had a cold and imperious look about him, like a lizard. He drew on his cigar with a self-important tilt of his head. His clothes and deportment were calculated to impress those around him. However, his affectations had the disagreeable effect on Morwenna. No wonder Catherine was not attracted to him. Presently he returned to the party, without incident.

At five to twelve, a light came on in the bedroom above the study and Morwenna spotted a thin female face framed by the window. With a shudder, she realised it was a Mavis Nancarrow. She must have been in her late fifties by then. Mavis had died when Morwenna was five, so she remembered her grandmother mainly from old photographs. It was snowing now and tiny flakes swirled around and powdered the terrace. It looked like Mavis was watching the scene, as her face appeared every few minutes. Morwenna leaned in to the tree to ensure she could not be seen.

Soon after half past twelve, Catherine appeared around the side of the house. She had excused herself from the party, ostensibly to go to bed. She must have climbed the main staircase, collected her white fur cape from her bedroom, and then come down the back-stairs and exited by the kitchen door. She was a tall and graceful figure. As the light hit her face Morwenna noticed her chiselled features, wide mouth and high arched brows. Catherine wrapped the fur cape tightly around her as she limped onto the south terrace and positioned herself next to the railings. She only waited a few minutes before Jonathan came out of the front door to join her.

'Keep calm,' Morwenna whispered to herself, as her temples beat and a freezing dread gripped her stomach.

'Did anyone see you leave?' asked Catherine nervously.

'No, and I'd better not be too long,' said Jonathan moodily. 'What do you want?'

'I wanted to say sorry, really I am. I won't tell Emily about us, I promise,' said Catherine. 'I was just being childish.'

Jonathan struck a match and lit a cigarette. He positioned himself next to Catherine, looking more at ease. After a thoughtful pause, he drew on his cigarette and replied, 'thanks Cathy. I've been worrying all week that you might have told her already. I am grateful.'

'I can do better than *you* anyway,' laughed Catherine, her haughty chin in the air, 'I mean to do something special with my life. Maybe even form a band, like the Beatles. I don't want to be tied to a provincial bank manager.'

Jonathan became watchful again and kept glancing at the front door as they were talking, but Catherine appeared relaxed with her back resting on the railings.

'Don't stay out here too long Cathy. You'll freeze to death,' said Jonathan over his shoulder, as he stubbed out his cigarette and headed back to the party.

'I'm just going to have a ciggy myself and then go up to bed,' she called. 'You know Edith doesn't like me smoking in the bedroom. She thinks I'll to burn the house down!'

Catherine leant against the railings and her foot slid slightly forward on the ice. Morwenna cringed, maybe this had been an accident after all.

Unexpectedly, a female figure appeared from the kitchen garden. She was wearing a long leopard-print coat, a fur hat and matching gloves. *Mavis Nancarrow*, Morwenna thought to herself. Morwenna assumed that Mavis must have seen Catherine and Jonathan together from her bedroom window.

'Hi Mavis, what are you doing out here? I thought you had a headache.'

'Not at all Cathy. I heard you arranging to meet Jonathan earlier, and I've been watching you two from my bedroom. I wanted a little chat with you.'

Morwenna glanced at her watch which read twenty to one. Titan produced a low growl in his throat and his mistress silenced him by resting her hand on his head. She gripped his collar tight. She didn't want him running off, so she gave him another dog-treat.

'Don't tell anyone about Jonathan and I,' pleaded Catherine. 'It's finished anyway.'

'I'm not interested in your pathetic boyfriends,' hissed Mavis. Her look was threatening and she leaned towards the younger woman.

'What's the matter?' asked Catherine, looking very alarmed. Her stance stiffened and she gripped the railing.

'I can't believe Frank has been so stupid and weak since you came to Gwedr Iowarth. I told him to deal with this years ago. You do know you are Edith's daughter, don't you?' spat Mavis, moving even closer to Catherine with strangled rage.

'You're mistaken. It's impossible,' said Catherine in a stifled tone.

'Edith tricked Jory into inheriting his fortune. I can't believe that Frank was disinherited for gambling and Edith inherited all of this, when she had secretly become pregnant with *you* during the War. I'm not having Ebrel deprived of her rightful inheritance by you,' Mavis barked and jabbed Catherine in the chest.

'We should ask Edith,' said Catherine shakily, 'I think you must be mistaken. Let's go inside.'

Catherine was cornered against the railings and seemingly over-whelmed by the Mavis's revelations. Morwenna had an urge to alert the young woman, but she knew she mustn't.

'I have proof. Frank gave me the evidence yesterday. Look at this!' said Mavis, taking a piece of paper out of her pocket.

Mavis unfolded the paper and suddenly flung it towards Catherine's face. Her victim screamed in pain, raising her hands to her eyes. With one fluid movement, Mavis reached towards Catherine's ankles with her right hand and pushed the young woman in the chest with her left hand. Catherine screamed and disappeared over the cliff. Morwenna closed her eyes in shock and inadvertently released Titan from her grasp.

The wind took away Catherine's screams and the dog charged towards Mavis. Titan took a massive leap and knocked the top off the bird bath, which went crashing to the ground. He landed behind Mavis and clamped his jaw below her knee, just for a moment. Titan was not a naturally bad-tempered canine and he soon released the villain.

'Bloody dog Athena, I can't believe you bit me and how the hell did you get out here?' exclaimed Mavis while clasping the back of her leg to stem the flow of blood.

Morwenna could see dark fluid oozing from the back of Mavis's stockinged calf and leaking onto her glove. Titan was satisfied with the damage he had inflicted on his victim, and he slunk back to his mistress. The dog was concerned that he could be in trouble after his ferocious exploits.

Mavis placed her hand in the hollow base of the bird bath and then, with some considerable effort, she lifted the top back into place. She glanced around her and limped back towards the kitchen garden, presumably to return to her bedroom via the kitchen and the back-stairs.

Morwenna retched a few times and resisted the temptation to leave her hiding place and look down onto the rocks. Stillness prevailed and snowflakes drifted over the offending footprints. The only sound she could hear now was her heart drumming against her ribs. Morwenna deliberately slowed her breathing and allowed a little time for her racing pulse to settle and her body to stop shaking. She found some solace in hoping Catherine's death had been swift. Titan snuggled up to her and she hugged him close. She couldn't resist giving him another dog-treat to reward him for biting Mavis.

As expected, Phillipe was the next to emerge from the house. He sauntered to his sports car. He was waved-off by Edith at about one o'clock. As Emily described, Emily and Dr Watson chatted for a while and drove off about one fifteen. They were blissfully unaware of Catherine's murder.

Morwenna neither moved nor loosened her hold on Titan's collar for another twenty minutes. This action was partly to calm herself and partly to ensure everyone was in bed before she proceeded with the second part of her plan, the details of which she hadn't told Harriet. Morwenna walked around the perimeter of the house to ensure all the lights were extinguished. She didn't return to the mirror but kept moving until she reached the kitchen garden from the other side.

It was dark there and Morwenna put the torch back on. She tried the back door which was locked. She swiftly unlocked it, with the spare key she had in her pocket. She and Titan entered the kitchen to be met by a very inquisitive Athena, who barked a few times and wagged her tail vigorously. Morwenna hoped Athena wouldn't give them away. She gave the female dog some food-treats and stroked her rough head to keep her quiet. Titan and Athena sniffed each other but they didn't make a big fuss.

'Meet your great, great grandmother,' said Morwenna to Titan. She then turned to Athena and whispered, 'Sorry you got the blame for biting Mavis!'

The two dogs accompanied Morwenna, as she left the kitchen. She peered around the door and gingerly picked her way across the hall towards the sitting room. On entering, she moved directly to the sideboard and extracted the key for the grandfather clock from the secret drawer. She unlocked the glass door and opened it. Morwenna read the time and date by torch light, *quarter to two on 1st January 1963*. She opened the bottom of the clock and grasped the pendulum to stop it. She moved the hands to read eleven o'clock and set the date dial to

28th May 2020. She loosened the nuts holding the clock face in place, using the wrench. Morwenna took the pot of glue from her pocket and unscrewed it. With her right hand she flexed the clock face forward and with her left she poured the adhesive into the mechanism behind. Titan and Athena looked at her curiously and she gave them a couple more dog-treats to keep them busy. She re-locked the glass door and returned the keys to their drawer.

Next Morwenna crept to Edith's study, realising she needed to find a way to make sure Edith didn't have the clock mended. Morwenna took a piece of writing paper and penned the following letter:

Dear Edith,

I'm so sorry for your loss. I can't tell you the name of the murderer because it would be dangerous to alter the course of history. But I promise to give you this information before you die. Don't have the grandfather clock mechanism mended as it acts as a time portal and it will allow me to inform you of the truth, when I can safely do so.

Love,

Morwenna (2020)

Morwenna placed the letter in an envelope and put it in the top drawer of Edith's desk. She looked cautiously out of the study door, to check no one was in the hall, and then crept back to the kitchen. Athena had befriended Titan and she wanted to come with them. Morwenna had a little tussle with Athena, pushing her back into the kitchen, while keeping Titan with her. She locked the kitchen door from the outside and made her way back to the mirror. She glanced at her watch which read quarter past two. Morwenna and Titan slid through the mirror with ease and arrived back in 2020.

'Why did you take so long?' shouted Harriet as Morwenna re-appeared on the 2020 side of the mirror.

'I had to tie up a few loose ends,' said Morwenna. 'Jonathan is innocent, thank goodness. Mavis Nancarrow pushed Catherine over the railings.'

'Blimey that's a relief,' said Harriet in a milder tone. 'I tried to follow you through the mirror but I couldn't.'

Morwenna soon warmed up on the balmy summer evening in 2020 and she shed her fur coat and the two women returned the house. They sat in the study while Morwenna gave Harriet a blow-by-blow account of her adventure, over a glass of brandy. Harriet insisted on hearing every last detail and they finally went to bed at about quarter to four.

Chapter 23

The Reveal

Naturally both Harriet and Morwenna struggled to wake up the next morning. By the time they arose, after ten o'clock, Natalie was making good progress preparing sandwiches and cake for Ada's leaving party. Thankfully it was a sunny day, so they could hold the event outside. It was still illegal to have indoor gatherings due to the pandemic. Harriet and Morwenna had agreed that Harriet would use the occasion to announce the identity of the murderer and give an explanation of why the crime happened.

'We know the murderer and we know why she did it. But we still can't prove it or explain the timing,' said Morwenna. 'We can't tell them about the time travel or they will think we're bonkers.'

'Don't worry,' said Harriet. 'I have everything I need to prove the identity of the murderer and to explain why the murder took place at that exact moment. Everything can be proven from the evidence we have here, in 2020. The time-travel need never be mentioned.'

'Tell *me* then,' implored Morwenna.

'All in good time. I'll tell you when I tell everyone else,' replied Harriet tapping the side of her nose and looking very self-satisfied.

Harriet wanted to put on a theatrical performance. She placed photographs of Edith, Frank Nancarrow, Mavis Nancarrow, Ebrel Trevethan, Morgan Trevethan, Jonathan and Phillipe Bouvier on the table. Harriet carried the blackboards from the library and she placed a freezer bag and a pair of kitchen tongs on the table by Ada's presents.

'What on earth do you need those for?' asked Morwenna.

'The evidence,' replied Harriet without giving any further explanation.

Everything was in place by midday. Morwenna kept trying to contact Jonathan by phone but she was still having no success, when their party guests started to arrive. Natalie had prepared a variety of cocktails and Morwenna was making cups of tea. Angela Smalley arrived first from the solicitor's office and she was soon followed by Emily Watson. Emily looked at ease straight away, chatting cordially with Angela about Angela's father whom Emily knew well.

Joseph Penhaligon wore his best and only suit. He slipped awkwardly into the vacant chair at the far end of the terrace. Titan was nervous among crowds and Morwenna was busy, so he joined Joseph who patted him affectionately. Joseph sat rather timidly although he nodded politely to people he knew. He was not accustomed to social gatherings, so he tried to remain unobtrusive. Soon after Natalie's mother, Glenda, arrived and a couple of other ladies from the village. Glenda made a point of speaking with Joseph and Morwenna was glad that she was treating him kindly.

After the guests finished their food, Morwenna delivered a thoughtful speech thanking Ada for her years of service. Ada became quite tearful when she was presented with the selection of books from the library. The audience applauded in appreciation.

The cheers lessened. Harriet rose and clapped her hands, as a sign she was going to proceed with *her* part of the presentation. The guests settled down and looked on expectantly. A dignified hush advanced through the onlookers.

'Nearly fifty years ago a young woman called Catherine Nicholas lost her life by falling from this terrace,' said Harriet dramatically and pointing to the railings. 'After Morwenna and I came here we discovered that Edith Nancarrow believed that this wasn't an accident and that Catherine had been murdered. We have spent the last few weeks investigating this crime. I can tell you that we have pinpointed the murderer with certainty and we have the evidence to prove their identity, beyond all reasonable doubt,' said Harriet to a shocked and attentive audience.

At that moment, a taxi drew up and Jonathan Coutts stepped out. Morwenna walked towards the car and there was some frantic whispering.

'There will be a brief interlude in our proceedings,' said Harriet to her spectators, as she thought that was the most tactful thing to do. The onlookers talked uncomfortably amongst themselves, to avoid an embarrassing silence. It was several minutes before Jonathan sat down with Morwenna, who looked slightly flustered. Harriet nodded to Jonathan, but she was not daunted and resumed her monologue.

'All the suspects for this murder are either here in person or represented by their photograph,' continued Harriet. 'At the start the only person we could really exclude was Edith Nancarrow as she had no motive to kill Catherine and she had written to Morwenna, before she died, asking for this investigation. The problem we had, was that every one of our suspects had both motive and opportunity.

Could it have been Ada, the jealous maid who subsequently benefitted from Edith's will? We know Emily Watson had found out about her fiancé, Jonathan, kissing Catherine on Christmas Eve. Perhaps she had a fit of jealous rage? Phillipe Bouvier had a history of aggression to women and he had been rejected by Catherine.

Maybe Jonathan Coutts killed Catherine, to silence her threats to tell Emily about their relationship? Unbeknown to the family, Edith had left all her money and this house to Catherine. Perhaps one of the relatives had discovered this from the solicitor and they wanted Catherine dead to ensure their branch of the family inherited later, when Edith Nancarrow died? This could have been a motive for Frank, Mavis, Ebrel or Morgan. Finally, Joseph Penhaligon was struggling with illness. Possibly he took Catherine's life when he was suffering with troubling symptoms or under the influence of psychiatric drugs?'

Her audience was silent and the onlookers strained to hear to everything that Harriet had to say.

'In the end it was the *timing* of this murder which was absolutely crucial. Why did Catherine need to die at this particular time? After all, she had been living at Gwedr Iowarth for seven years and our suspects had plenty of previous opportunities to kill her. There are several crucial elements here. This is a tale about the strength of a mother's love for a daughter and it was all to do with the *feet*.

'*The feet?*' questioned Ada.

'Yes Ada. It was *you* who told me that Edith never let anyone see her feet,' continued Harriet. 'You informed me that Edith had webbed toes. On each foot her second and third toes were joined together by a web of skin. This is medically referred to as syndactyly. While it is normal for aquatic animals such as ducks and frogs to have webbed toes, it is not common among humans. Webbed toes are said to occur in approximately one out of every two thousand births. The toes most commonly attached are the second and third.

The condition is inherited and family members often share the trait. Of course, Morwenna also has webbed toes, which we might expect since she is Edith's great niece. You will remember Catherine was out walking with Frank Nancarrow the day before New Year's Eve. She slipped on the rocks and cut her foot rather badly. Frank had to remove her shoe to stem the bleeding. He noticed Catherine had webbed toes and he realised Catherine was Edith's daughter. He was Edith's older brother and he had seen her toes many times as a child.'

'So, Frank killed Catherine?' asked Jonathan, unable to restrain himself.

'No Frank Nancarrow was weak and bitter but he was no killer. That evening he told his wife, Mavis, about his discovery that Catherine was Edith's child. Mavis was furious. She had married Frank in the full expectation of inheriting Gwedr Iowarth and the family fortune when Jory Nancarrow died. Frank was disinherited for gambling because Jory his father had strong Victorian values. Edith had inherited the house and the fortune, in spite of becoming pregnant whilst unmarried during the War. Mavis knew she and Frank would be unlikely to inherit from Edith, who was much younger, but she wanted to ensure Catherine was out of the way so Ebrel would inherit when Edith died. Mavis had suffered several miscarriages and she was not going to let her only daughter miss out. Edith, on the other hand, had kept Catherine's identity a secret to try and protect her.'

'It's a perfect theory,' said Emily, 'but how can it be proven. How did Mavis know Catherine would be on the terrace and how did an older woman overcome a youngster and push her to her death?'

Harriet picked up her plastic bag and the kitchen tongs. She walked towards the bird table and, with a good deal of effort, removed the top to expose the hollow base.

'You will all remember that the pepper-pot went missing on the night of the murder and was never found,' announced Harriet with a flourish.

The pepper-pot was hidden in the hollow base of the bird bath, as Harriet expected. She placed the tongs around the pepper-pot, to avoid contaminating her evidence, and pulled it out. She dropped the article deftly into the freezer bag and sealed it.

'There won't be finger prints on it, Harriet,' said Morwenna if Mavis was wearing gloves, after all it was a freezing winter night.'

'Absolutely. There won't be finger prints but, the pepper-pot is covered with Mavis's blood,' explained Harriet.

Harriet passed the bag around the observers so they could observe the dried blood.

'Mavis retired to bed early on New Year's Eve, giving the excuse of a headache,' continued Harriet. 'She had overheard Jonathan and Catherine planning to meet on the terrace and she spotted her opportunity. Mavis was in the bedroom above the study and she watched Catherine on the south terrace meeting briefly with Jonathan. Once Jonathan returned inside, Mavis came down the back-stairs and took the pepper-pot from the kitchen table. She removed the stopper and emptied the contents into a piece of paper. She placed the empty pepper-pot in one pocket and the folded paper containing the pepper in the other. Mavis accosted Catherine on the terrace, indicated she needed to show her something and then threw the pepper into her victim's face. While Catherine was incapacitated, it was easy to push her over the railings, which were much lower in those days. Remember, Mavis told everyone the next day Athena, the deerhound, had bitten her. It was true she had been bitten. After Mavis killed Catherine, the dog ran at her, knocking the top off the bird bath and bit the back of her leg. She touched her leg to assess the damage and spilled blood on her gloves. She then dropped the pepper-pot in the base of the bird bath and put the top back on.'

'Surely, she would have retrieved the pepper-pot, if it had her blood on it, in case it was ever found?' asked Natalie.

'She would have reclaimed the pepper-pot if she had touched it with her bare hands, as the police could match finger-prints in those days, but she wore gloves. Mavis wouldn't worry about the blood, as DNA testing hadn't been invented in 1963. Over the following few days, the house was being searched by police so Mavis decided it was too risky to try and retrieve it,' explained Harriet. 'To be absolutely sure, I've arranged to have the blood sample checked against Morwenna's DNA, to prove it was her grandmother's.'

'It's a shame Edith will never know that you solved this,' said Ada.

'Maybe she can see us now?' reflected Morwenna. 'I'd like to think she has found her peace.'

After Harriet's speech, the guests drifted away. Natalie and Ada went into the kitchen to tidy up. Harriet packaged a sample of the dried blood in a test-tube, to be dropped off at Truro hospital for DNA analysis. Morwenna and Jonathan were left alone on the south terrace.

'I wasn't expecting you back so soon,' said Morwenna.

'I knew you wouldn't be able to leave this alone,' answered Jonathan, pointing his finger towards the grounds of Gwedr Iowarth. 'I needed to come back, to explain. I cut the outback tour short and flew home as soon as I received a negative test for corona virus.'

'Thank God you weren't the murderer. Tell me truthfully Jonathan. Did you know I was Edith's great niece when we met?' asked Morwenna.

'Honestly, I had no idea. I had forgotten Mavis Nancarrow's daughter had married a man with the surname Trevethan. I only realised the connection three months after we got together, when I recognised your father in a photograph album. I thought about telling you countless times but it seemed pointless. I thought Edith must have died years ago. After I left Gwedr Iowarth in 1963, I went to London and tried to forget about all of this. I never quite recovered from Edith believing I was a suspect and Emily dumping me straight away,' explained Jonathan.

Morwenna was tempted to tell Jonathan about the time-travel, and that she needed to go back one more time and meet Edith, but she decided to keep it a secret for the time being. After all, Jonathan had kept quite a lot of information from her. She definitely had the upper-hand in terms of having her own way, keeping Gwedr Iowarth and Titan.

'I believe you,' said Morwenna, 'but I'm telling you now. We are staying in Cornwall and I'm keeping Titan!'

'It's a deal,' said Jonathan, looking relieved.

Reunited with her husband at Gwedr Iowarth, her former suspicion that he was a murderer seemed absurd. Morwenna felt guilty for doubting him, albeit in her darkest moments. A feeling of calm returned and Titan trotted up to lick Jonathan's hand.

'My goodness, he likes me,' said Jonathan.

'You two are going to get along just fine,' concluded Morwenna.

Chapter 24

Goodbye to Ada

The next morning Ada descended the *main* staircase with her suitcase, having spent her last night in Catherine's old room. She paused on the bottom step and surveyed the hall from the perspective of a visitor. The housekeeper closed her eyes, smelling the air which held long familiar tones of beeswax polish and roses. For a moment, she heard the echo of music and chatter from a bygone age. The house was ready for change and new, happier memories. Ada's anxiety gave way to excitement and she moved forward with her head held high. She placed her suitcase by the front door, as she intended to leave that way.

Harriet was conscious that Morwenna and Jonathan needed to have time alone, so she suggested that she would drive Ada to Falmouth, via the supermarket, and Natalie would come along to help.

It was strange leaving Ada in Falmouth, knowing she would not be living at Gwedr Iowarth anymore. Harriet and Natalie checked the phone, water, heating and electric were fully functional before they finally tore themselves away. They left Ada experimenting with the new computer, sitting proudly in her sitting room.

'I'm so glad you weren't the murderer Ada,' called Harriet, smiling as they left. 'Although it was touch and go for a while. We did have you on our list of suspects.'

'The furniture suited the house well,' giggled Natalie as they drove away,' but I wasn't keen on her choice of floral curtains and furniture coverings.'

'Yes, the décor was a bit loud. It'll be really strange for her over the next few days,' reflected Harriet. 'I suspect Ada has rarely spent a night alone in her entire life. We must phone her regularly for the first few weeks.'

'Changing the subject,' said Natalie. 'What's Jonathan like?'

'He's a lovely guy,' said Harriet. 'Very quiet, but what he says counts. It sounds harsh to say it, but for a while all the evidence pointed towards him.'

Once Natalie and Harriet returned to Gwedr Iowarth, Natalie slipped outside to continue hauling her, newly delivered turf from the drive to the tennis court. It needed to be laid and watered before it dried out. Although it was extremely hard work, pushing barrow loads of turf, she enjoyed the exertion associated with intense physical work. Harriet found Morwenna and Jonathan sitting at the kitchen table. Thankfully both appeared untroubled. Jonathan had decided to take the car back to Bath so he could collect some clothes and things Morwenna wanted from the flat. Jonathan had been coaxed into placing their Bath property on the market and moving to Cornwall permanently.

'Jonathan has agreed to move to Gwedr Iowarth,' announced Morwenna with an approving smile.

'Brilliant news,' said Harriet who couldn't help feeling a little jealous. Now that Jonathan was here, Harriet had a feeling she should make plans to leave. She was delighted things were good between Morwenna and Jonathan but she had enjoyed having Morwenna to herself. She felt uncharacteristically proprietorial about Gwedr Iowarth and the adventures they had there.

'I suppose I should return to Edward and Aaron in Wales,' said Harriet referring to her husband and son.

Aaron had been attending university *online* and Edward was keeping him company, while Harriet was in Cornwall.

'Absolutely not,' said Morwenna. 'If Aaron has finished studying for this term, they should come down here for a holiday. There is plenty of space. Also, you know I hate cooking!'

'Great idea Wenna. I think they would enjoy a change of scene,' replied Harriet.

Harriet cooked a Spanish omelette for lunch. Natalie came inside, red in the face, after her efforts moving turf.

'It's a massive job moving *all* that turf on my own,' pleaded Natalie.

'After lunch, we'll come outside and give you a hand,' said Morwenna, winking at Harriet.

Morwenna waved Jonathan off and reminded him to bring the tennis racquets. He intended to return the following day, after he had checked the flat and retrieved the items his wife had requested. Natalie returned to her mammoth task of moving turf. Morwenna arrived back into the kitchen just in time to help Harriet with the clearing-up.

'I'm going through the mirror for the last time tonight,' announced Morwenna, turning to Harriet and gesturing towards the garden with her soapy hands.

'I thought you might,' said Harriet. 'But is it really necessary?'

'It is now. After I saw Mavis push Catherine off the cliff, I returned to the house and set the grandfather clock for 28th May 2020, the night before Edith died. I realised my movements through the mirror are tied to the time on the clock. So, I made sure the clock was frozen at the time I need. I also wrote a letter to Edith promising I would tell her who the culprit was.'

'But why return to the evening of her death?' asked Harriet.

'Blimey Harriet, I thought you were the super-sleuth! I need to tell Edith who killed Catherine, at a time it can't alter history. It was you that impressed upon me that I shouldn't change the past. This gives me the best of all eventualities. I'll have the opportunity to meet Edith, and she learns the truth before she dies,' explained Morwenna.

'Will you take Titan?' asked Harriet.

'That would mean Titan would meet himself two months ago. That's weird even by my standards as a veteran time traveller!' said Morwenna. 'No, I'll leave Titan behind, this time.'

'I guess we'd better help Natalie move that turf,' said Harriet once the dishes were dried and put away.

Even though Natalie had already worked hard, there was still a huge pile of turf by the drive. Morwenna found a second wheelbarrow in the summer house which meant she and Harriet could move the turf while Natalie laid it. A few days earlier, Natalie and Joseph had removed the net posts and hired a digger to lift the old turf. A couple of tonnes of fine top-soil mixed with sand had been deposited on the court and they had spent several days rolling it. They used an ancient roller and a spirit level to make the ground as flat as possible. Joseph had repaired and oiled the posts and a new tension-wire and net had been delivered.

Natalie was now going over the soil with a fine rake and laying the turf behind her. She had to speak to Titan firmly to banish him from the court, so he charged around the adjacent lawn instead. He was like a fool that afternoon, galloping in circles and snapping at insects. A good deal of huffing and puffing went on until Harriet decided they needed a break and a drink.

Harriet brought the lemonade outside. She and Morwenna flopped onto the grass, exhausted from their endeavours. Natalie stood admiring her handywork with her hands on her hips. Titan prodded her with his nose, urging her to play with him. He had found a very old tennis ball when Joseph brought the net posts out of the summer house. Natalie threw the ball for the dog and, when he returned it, she rolled on the floor with him and wrestled it from his mouth. Eventually Natalie needed a rest too and she collapsed onto the ground next to the others.

'When will we be able to play tennis? asked Morwenna.

'I think the new turf will need a month to bed down with regular rolling, cutting and watering,' explained Natalie.

'We can have a tennis tournament in August,' said Harriet eagerly. 'We'll have plenty of participants, Jonathan, Edward, me, you two and Aaron. That's six of us altogether, brilliant.'

'You'll like Aaron, Natalie. He's about your age,' explained Morwenna. 'He's not as loud as his mother!'

'I haven't played on a grass court since we used to play away at Lunesdale,' reminisced Morwenna, looking at Harriet. 'Remember they had grass courts. They were pretty rough those courts. Sometimes the cows escaped from the field and left cow-pats on them.'

'My courts will be finely manicured,' said Natalie grandly. 'Similar to Wimbledon!'

'Thank goodness for that,' said Morwenna. 'On the Lunesdale courts you had to volley most shots to avoid letting the ball bounce!'

Harriet returned inside at five o'clock to make preparations for dinner. She was grateful to escape from wheeling the turf as her arms and legs were aching. It seemed relatively light work to chop the chicken and vegetables for a stir-fry, in comparison. Harriet wished she could accompany Morwenna to the past, just once. Harriet was used to being more daring than Morwenna and she was becoming frustrated with having to hear about her friend's exploits and not participate in them.

Later Morwenna and Natalie appeared at the kitchen door, with Titan. They looked exhausted and filthy. They each drank a pint of water and retreated upstairs to wash and change out of their work clothes. Harriet rinsed the rice, put that to one side and set the wok on the stove. She was cooking chicken with green pepper and black-bean sauce. Now Ada had left, she could prepare a more adventurous menu. She set the kitchen table, as eating there seemed more convivial than the formal dining room. This arrangement also avoided the inconvenience of passing plates through the hatch.

Natalie, Morwenna and Harriet sat companionably around the kitchen table and they soon polished off a bottle of white wine with the stir-fry. Natalie had missed the food preparation, so she insisted Harriet describe the 'recipe' and she recorded it neatly in her folder.

'It was invented really,' said Harriet. 'It's baking where you have to follow the instructions more accurately. It's just a case of following the basics for the main course. You only need to be able to cook about ten dishes and you can adapt them for variety.'

'How can I save time?' asked Natalie, 'to spend more time in the garden.'

'I'm no chef,' said Morwenna, 'but I am a big believer in batch cooking. If you make a lasagne, make three and freeze the other two. In that way you only need to cook three of four times a week.'

'I definitely like the sound of that,' replied the new housekeeper.

Natalie cleared up after dinner and the two older women took Titan for a walk. Morwenna was feeling concerned that she wouldn't be able to take Titan to see Edith.

'I wouldn't feel guilty Wenna,' said Harriet. 'When you think about it. He'll be there already!'

'You're right, Harri,' replied Morwenna. 'Time travel is so weird. In some ways I'm glad this is the last time I'm going to do it.'

Natalie was exhausted and she retired early to watch TV in her room, so Harriet and Morwenna were left to work out their evening escapade in private.

'I haven't really *made* a plan for tonight,' explained Morwenna. 'I think I'll take a lead from Great Aunt Edith and go with the flow, so to speak. I set the grandfather clock for eleven o'clock, so I'll travel through the mirror just before that.'

'I'll wait up with you,' said Harriet. 'It's a bit like waiting at an airport, isn't it? The time really drags before your time-travel adventures.'

Chapter 25

Meeting Great Aunt Edith

Just before eleven, that evening, Harriet and Morwenna proceeded into the garden. They took the spare back door key with them. Titan was unhappy being locked in the kitchen and woofed a few times, but Morwenna couldn't risk the unknown consequences of Titan meeting himself. The two women approached the mirror, and as Morwenna stepped through, Harriet hung onto her arm and they travelled together. To her amazement Harriet found herself on the other side and it was late spring.

'Oh, my goodness, you came through. Well done!' said Morwenna.

Harriet whooped with joy and excitement and Morwenna suggested she, *pipe-down,* before they woke Ada. She would probably call the police and raise Joseph Penhaligon from his bed, if she heard them. Harriet wore her most contrite expression as she followed her companion noiselessly. The two women made their way to the rear of the house and unlocked the back door.

The kitchen was almost the same as the one they left a few minutes earlier. It was deathly still except for the ticking of the mantle clock and the central-heating boiler emitting its familiar rumble. Harriet placed her finger to her lips and nodded towards Ada's sitting room. The door stood open. Harriet tiptoed slowly across the kitchen and she cautiously peered inside to check the housekeeper hadn't fallen asleep in the armchair. Thankfully the room was empty except for Ada's furniture.

'I hope Titan doesn't give us away,' whispered Harriet, as they crossed the kitchen and prepared to enter the hall.

'We could use the back-stairs, but we risk meeting Ada and that would be far worse,' said Morwenna in a low voice. 'No, we'll go up the main staircase.'

Titan was lying in the hall with his head on the bottom step. He looked disinterestedly at Harriet and Morwenna and turned his head away as they ascended the stairs. Ada's words from a few weeks ago came back to Morwenna, *Titan usually ignores people the first time he meets them.* Of course, as far as Titan was concerned this was his initial meeting with her. On Morwenna's first day at Gwedr Iowarth, the dog had already met her on the 28th May 2020, hence he greeted her as a friend.

The two hunched women inched up the stairs, trying to make no noise. They cringed as the steps creaked beneath their shoes and, at the top, turned intuitively towards Edith's door. Morwenna glanced at her watch which read quarter past eleven and she tentatively knocked.

'Come in, Morwenna,' barked a confident voice which was more powerful than they had expected. Morwenna and Harriet looked at each other in surprise, and the two women entered the room with a degree of trepidation.

'Well, you cut it a bit fine, didn't you,' exclaimed Edith from the four-poster bed, 'and there's two of you. I wasn't expecting that!'

They crossed the room, to approach the old lady. Her body was quite tiny and her face gaunt, but Edith's shrewd amber eyes gleamed in the darkness. Morwenna felt Edith's gaze upon her and her companion.

'Pull up another chair. I only expected Morwenna, so I set *one* seat by the bed and that was difficult enough!' proclaimed Edith brightly and she nodded at Morwenna. 'I needn't ask who you are but who do you have with you?'

'This is Harriet Duncan, my friend and chief investigator,' said Morwenna. 'She has been invaluable in solving Catherine's murder. I identified the murderer but Harriet found the pepper-pot with the murderer's blood on it and she cleverly solved the mystery of why the murderer killed Catherine at that *specific* time.'

'Well done, Morwenna,' said Edith, 'and don't think I've forgiven you for pouring glue down the mechanism of my grandfather clock. That was a valuable family heirloom. I guess *you* can have it mended now?'

'Sorry about the clock, but stopping it *permanently* became a necessity. Where shall I start?' asked Morwenna.

'Well, I've worked one thing out. I'm going to die tonight, or before the morning,' said Edith. 'So, don't worry about protecting my feelings. I suggest you start with the culprit and then we can have a nice long chat about anything we like.'

'The murderer was my grandmother,' said Morwenna bluntly.

'Doesn't surprise me,' retorted Edith. 'Did you know Mavis?'

'Only slightly,' replied Morwenna. 'I was very young when she died. I'll let Harriet explain how Mavis discovered Catherine was your daughter which prompted what happened afterwards.'

The old lady listened intently while Harriet explained about Catherine's webbed toes and how these had been inherited from Edith. When Catherine cut her foot on the rocks, Frank Nancarrow saw she had webbed toes and made the natural connection that Catherine was Edith's daughter.

'That explains why Catherine never went swimming. She wouldn't show her feet to anyone,' said Edith, nodding her head. 'I didn't believe she was frightened of water because she was so fearless about everything else.'

'Frank told Mavis that Catherine was your daughter,' explained Harriet in a steady tone. 'Mavis was furious that you had got away with having an illegitimate baby, as she saw it. She was bitter that you had inherited Gwedr Iowarth, by deceiving your father. She was determined to remove Catherine from the picture, so Ebrel would inherit at a later date. Mavis overheard Jonathan and Catherine arranging to meet, on the south terrace, during the party. She feigned a headache so she could watch them from her room. Then she went down the backstairs as soon as Jonathan left.'

'How did Mavis have the strength to overcome Catherine. She would have put up a hell of a fight?' said Edith.

'That's where the pepper-pot came in. Mavis threw pepper in

186

Catherine's face and hid the blood-stained pepper pot in the base of the bird bath and we found it,' explained Harriet. 'The pepper-pot had Mavis's blood on it because she touched the back of her leg where the dog had bitten her. I sent the blood for DNA analysis.'

'I always thought it was odd that Athena bit Mavis. Athena had never attacked anyone before,' said Edith.

'It wasn't Athena that bit Mavis,' admitted Morwenna. 'It was Titan. I took him back in time with me to help solve the murder.'

'Ah, I understand,' said Edith. 'Good for Titan, best dog I ever had. You told me the grandfather clock sets the time portal, but how do you actually leave the present?'

'Through the mirror, by the summer house,' replied Harriet.

'All those mirrors are weird,' said Edith. 'I keep away from them. I used to experience a strange feeling when I looked through them. Like I could see shadows from the past. After Catherine died, I encouraged William Penhaligon to let the shrubs grow around the edge of the garden to cover them up.'

'Great Aunt Edith,' asked Morwenna. 'Can we ask *you* a few questions?'

'*Great Aunt*, that makes me sound *really* old,' said Edith.

'Well, you are a hundred,' laughed her great-niece.

'Of course, I'll answer your questions. How selfish of me. You have worked hard and taken all sorts of risks, so I can die knowing the truth. Go ahead,' said Edith brightly.

'What happened to Catherine's father?'

Edith explained that Catherine's father had been called Nathanial Thomas. The story was not uncommon. Edith had been working in the Land Army in the spring of 1943 and she had met Nathanial at a dance in Halton near Lancaster. He was there for a few weeks and he knew of Edith's pregnancy before he left.

'He was married, of course, so he could do nothing to help. We didn't love each other anyway,' said Edith without sentiment. 'When Catherine died, my private investigator traced his work address in Alabama and I wrote to him. He wrote a lovely letter back and he admitted he thought of me sometimes and he wondered about the baby. His wife never knew and I thought that was best. It would have been pointless to wreck another family's happiness.'

Edith and Morwenna chatted for a while, after all they had over fifty years of news to exchange. Harriet thought it was so sad they hadn't been friends for years, as they got along so well. Harriet wasn't used to keeping quiet but she felt privileged to be present, so she sat silently. She could find no words.

'Will you stay with me until I go?' asked Edith sleepily.

'Of course,' said Morwenna bravely.

'Look after Titan,' begged Edith.

'I promise,' whispered Morwenna. 'I wouldn't be without him now.'

After a while Edith's eyes closed and she slept peacefully. One side of her face dropped and her breathing became slower and more erratic. As Edith's soul slipped away, Harriet remained uncharacteristically still and restrained in the shadows.

Morwenna sat patiently holding Edith's hand until her breathing stopped altogether. She experienced a familiar burning sensation in her temple, from supressing her grief. For a few minutes, the two women lingered in their chairs, immobile and quiet with their own reflections of Edith's life. Neither of them cried outwardly.

Presently, they said their first and last goodbyes and stole out of the room. They crept down the stairs and Titan made a fuss of Morwenna and licked her hand, as she passed.

'See you in a few weeks Titan,' said Harriet.

The End

Printed in Great Britain
by Amazon